BELONG *to* YOU

#1 *New York Times* Bestselling Author
VI KEELAND

BELONG TO YOU: A COLE NOVEL

Edited by Ocean's Edge Editing
Cover photo:©CURAphotography Fotolia.com
Cover & Interior Formatting by Elaine York,
Allusion Graphics, LLC/Publishing & Book Formatting
www.allusiongraphics.com

To the boy who pushed me off my bicycle when we were six and scarred my knee. Who else would I dedicate this book to?

Chapter 1

"Can I get you something to drink?"

Startled out of my daydream by the perky flight attendant, it took me a minute to snap out of my thoughts. I was in such a fog that I couldn't be sure if I had just woken, and the last week had been just a dream, or if it was really an unforgettable memory.

"I'll have a vodka cranberry and she'll have a merlot. You'll have to excuse her, she's spent the last week fucking her brains out with a gorgeous stranger and can't seem to snap out of it." Sienna smiled to the appalled flight attendant, a pleasant-looking mid-forties woman who was wearing way too many pins on her bulging uniform. From the look on her face, I was sure the flight attendant wasn't used to a raunchy-mouth like Sienna in first class. I looked around and saw most of the other passengers looked well bred and refined, more like they were dressed for an uppity tennis match than a twelve hour flight from Honolulu to New York. Sienna would have stood out even if she didn't have a mouth like a truck driver.

Sienna McAllister had been my best friend since the third grade. We became kindred spirits on our first day in chorus when we realized we could sing in natural harmony together without so much as a beat of music. Twenty years later, our lives had taken us down very different paths, but it had never dulled our bond.

Aside from being the same age, we had nothing in common on the outside anymore. With her wild, dark curls falling around her alabaster skin, and black tight-fitting clothes coupled with five-inch laced-up leather boots, Sienna looked like she'd just walked out of a rock band. If her voluptuous curves straining her tight clothes weren't enough to catch an eye as she passed by, the hundred or so bracelets she wore halfway up her arms actually played a sweet jingle as she moved.

I, on the other hand, had a penchant for pink and all things girly. My long blonde hair was almost white after a week in the sun and stood in stark contrast to my deeply-tanned skin — and the wild woman sitting next to me. When I was younger, I hated my olive skin and bright blonde hair. It was an unusual combination to have such tan skin and natural blonde hair. Most people assumed I was a bottle blonde. My dad used to tell me that I was special because I bound together my mom's Swedish ancestry with his Italian heritage. But, as I suspected most kids did in their teens at some point, I wanted to look like someone else. It took me until I was in my late teens to stop fighting my looks and to learn to play them up.

The flight attendant brought us our drinks and scurried away with a hesitant smile. It was obvious she was trying to avoid hearing any more about our vacation, which Sienna would have surely divulged if given the opportunity. Sienna enjoyed shocking uptight people with her crass mouth. Watching them squirm was a sport for her.

Sienna raised her glass to me in a toast. "To the best damn honeymoon I've ever been on." I laughed and shook my head as we clinked glasses and both tipped our heads back to drink.

Chapter 2

One week earlier

A full day of sun after we landed left me exhausted. I must not have been thinking straight when I booked a direct overnight flight from New York to Honolulu. Did I really think I would land at 8am and feel fresh and relaxed, ready to take on the first day of my honeymoon? A two hour nap on the beach did nothing to shake off my jetlag, and by 8pm, as I was getting ready for a night out with Sienna, I had started to wonder what I had got myself into.

We arrived at the resort's Japanese restaurant and I silently reminded myself that I needed to eat, even though I was not very hungry at all. The last time I'd gone out drinking with Sienna without eating, Michael had to carry me up the stairs when I passed out face down on the floor in the kitchen. Hating that thoughts of Michael still uncontrollably filled my memory, I took a deep breath and pushed all thought of him out of my head, determined not to let him ruin our honeymoon even more than he already had.

After we ordered, a pretty waitress wearing a traditional red kimono delivered us drinks served in coconuts with cute little purple umbrellas. "Thank you, but we didn't order those," I said as she started to put the drinks in front of us. The waitress smiled at me and silently pointed to the other end of the restaurant where I saw a table of a dozen men, one of which was holding up a drink and smiling.

Sienna smiled and took one of the drinks and held it up, offering cheers back to the smiling man. Even though he was across the room, I could see he was handsome and had a damn sexy smile. My eyes scanned the table he was sitting at, and I almost gasped at what I took in. Damn, they were all handsome, one better looking than the next. They looked like they could have been traveling for a rugby tournament, or a Calvin Klein underwear photo shoot perhaps. I was grateful for my tan skin at that moment, so no one would see me blush.

Sienna clinked her glass to mine and said loud enough for the table next to us to hear, "Remember, we should do lots of fucking on our honeymoon, baby!" I choked on my drink before we laughed together like we were back in third grade.

Our dinner was just being served when I saw the boys club began to make their way out of the restaurant. Apparently, I wasn't the only one to notice their departure; they seemed to have the attention of half the restaurant. They were rowdy, handsome, and drinking a lot. The smiling man that had sent over our drinks stopped by our table with two of his friends on their way out. "I hope you ladies are coming down to the bonfire tonight that the resort is throwing." His dimpled smile made his face even more handsome.

"We are." Sienna raised her eyebrows and smiled up at the man. "And thank you for the drinks, they were delicious." Her response was more of a purr than a statement. I had forgotten how good at flirting she was. It was second nature to her. She had the ability to make anything sound teasing. I was pretty sure she could ask a man walking by for the time and he would think she wanted to sleep with him.

"You're very welcome. You know, this may sound like a bad pick-up line, but you look so familiar." His brows creased and I could see the wheels in motion as he tried to place her face.

Sienna raised one eyebrow provocatively. "Maybe we can figure out where you know me from at the bonfire later."

"Sounds like a good plan to me. " He smiled and I watched his eyes slowly drift over Sienna. But his attention was quickly called away by the rest of the boys club that were making a ruckus near the door. "I better go before the jackasses get themselves kicked out. I'll be looking for you ladies later."

After Sienna's brief time as the lead singer of No Worries, people always thought she looked familiar.

Five years ago the band had a number one hit, then they broke up due to fighting between the members before a follow up album could be released to cement their fame. Apparently the guitarist had been sleeping with the drummer's wife and they couldn't get past it. Unfortunately, the group became somewhat of a one hit wonder, but people still vaguely remembered Sienna's face. She really wasn't the type of woman that people forgot easily.

Sienna and I had played together in an all girl band in Boston for three years. We did a lot of local shows and had a pretty good following. It didn't earn us enough money to survive, but we loved doing it and it worked for us for a while. By the time we decided to go our separate ways, I had already met Michael and started pursuing a degree in music, slowly growing content with my life. Sienna hadn't given up on our dream of being rock stars, so we parted friends when she took off for New York at twenty-one to join No Worries as the lead singer.

After that, we talked on the phone twice a week and I went to New York to visit her on most of my breaks from school. There was definitely no love lost between her and Michael, and he made it clear that he disapproved of her partying lifestyle and didn't like my frequent trips to New York. I sacrificed a lot for Michael over the years, giving up a lot of who I was, but never let him come between Sienna and me. She was supposed to have been my maid of honor at our wedding last weekend.

Sienna watched as the boys club sauntered out of the restaurant and then turned to me. "Syd, I think you need to pick one of those boys and get a rebound screw under your belt. What better place to do it than Hawaii?"

"I told you, I don't feel ready to start dating yet." We had already had that conversation on the plane on the way to Hawaii, and I'd suspected Sienna had given up much too easily to have put the subject behind us.

"Who said anything about dating?" She smiled at me. "Just pick one out and have a great time. Don't think about it and don't overanalyze it. Fuck it, don't even find out his name. Just have fun, Syd. That Michael sucked the life out of my partner in crime and we are resurrecting her this week!"

I may not have been ready for a new guy, but I was definitely ready to go back to living my life and having fun. I responded to her speech with the only word that I knew would make her happy, other than agreeing with her. "Shots?"

Sienna squealed in delight and hugged me as she called the waiter over to order our tequila shots.

We were halfway between tipsy and drunk as we made our way down to the bonfire. It was a beautiful night and torches lit a path through the sand down to the water's edge. A huge bonfire was burning and a Caribbean calypso band played a song on steel drums with an older gentleman singing. Waiters floated around delivering fruity cocktails and women wearing bikini tops and hula skirts offered fresh flower leis.

I looked around and wasn't surprised to see that most of the partygoers were couples. After all, the resort was a favored honeymoon destination. It made me sad to think I was supposed to be there with Michael, relaxing after my wedding. Sienna picked up on the change in my mood and guided us to the large bar set up under the lights on the beach. "Two tequila shots please." Sienna's answer to every problem was always the same, tequila and a party. We drank back our shots, licked the salt off of the back of our hands and sucked our limes in unison.

"Another round for the ladies and all my friends, please." The deep velvety voice immediately sent a shiver up my spine. I turned to trace the voice to the face and was met with the most startling green eyes I had ever seen. I wasn't sure if it was the alcohol or the man, but I gasped and felt goose bumps breaking out on my arms. The eyes smiled down at me and I was momentarily unable to break the gaze. I blinked, forcing my eyes to escape the hold, and slowly looked down and realized that the captivating green eyes were attached to the most magnificent man I had ever seen, who was staring at me, watching me take him in. The corner of his perfect mouth turned up in a sexy half smile, and I knew he had just watched my body react to him. But he wasn't going to be a gentleman and pretend he didn't see it. Instead, he took a step closer into my personal space and I felt the heat radiate between us.

I turned back to the bartender to escape the intenseness of his glare and the bartender held out my next tequila shot. I twisted back around to thank the green-eyed god, and nearly slammed right into his chest. He had not moved out of my personal space. Instead he stood his ground and looked down at me, slightly amused. I held up my shot. "Are you joining me?"

"I'd love to." He smiled, but had no shot in his hand. He arched an eyebrow with a sexy grin on his face and I got the feeling that he wasn't accepting an offer to have a shot together. I laughed and shook my head before throwing back yet another shot, salt and lime. My head buzzed, and I knew I should probably stop drinking at that point, but I was thousands of miles from home with Sienna and that surely wouldn't be happening.

Sienna grabbed my hand and pulled me from the bar, oblivious to the beautiful creature standing behind me. "Come on, let's do one for old times' sake."

Only Sienna could talk a middle-aged Calypso band singer into letting us sing at the resort's welcome bonfire without knowing if we could even carry a tune. The last tequila shot went straight to my head and I was feeling no pain as I followed her to where the band was set up, anxious to sing with her. It had been years since we'd played together and I really did miss it.

Sienna spoke to the band and we sang one of our all time favorites, *Shake Your Body*, by the Jackson 5. It was a 70s boogie disco beat that people usually couldn't help but start to dance to. When we were done, people were applauding and dancing and the band asked us to do another song. What else could follow up a classic Jackson song but the Wild Cherry 70s hit, *Play That Funky Music?* Of course, we did our own version of the song, but people danced and sang along nonetheless. Even though it had been years since we'd performed together, no one would have guessed it. We worked together effortlessly, and it had been that way since that very first time in third grade. By the time we were done, the tequila had hit us with its full effect and we both laughed our way back to the bar, stumbling just a slight bit.

The bartender stopped pouring drinks as we approached and clapped his hands slowly for us, to which we responded with overzealous bows and a curtsy. He gave us each another shot of tequila on the house and we did our swallow, salt, lime routine in expert tandem. The handsome guy that had sent us drinks in the restaurant came over with a few of his friends.

"You ladies were amazing. That was incredible." He was smiling and it was obvious he was being sincere and it wasn't part of his pick up line.

"Thank you, it was so much fun!" Sienna responded, and I smiled. We were both on a post show high. It had been so long since I'd felt the familiar rush that I'd almost forgot what performing could do to me. We talked for a while and found out that the boys club wasn't actually in Hawaii for a rugby tournament or an underwear commercial shoot, they were there for a bachelor party.

"Wow, that's some bachelor party," I said to our new friend Tyler, the guy who'd bought us drinks in the restaurant.

"Yeah, the best man is loaded and is throwing the whole party. We have the penthouse for the week. Some of the guys are staying and others are going back in a few days. It's pretty sweet."

I actually felt, rather than saw, the green-eyed man return. I was positive that he was standing right behind me, but I couldn't bring myself to turn around and check. "Speak of the devil." Tyler pointed behind me and I slowly turned, finding the green-eyed god standing ridiculously close, staring down at me.

"Hi again." My words came out as a whisper. I could feel the heat radiating off his body and it was playing tricks on my brain that was swimming in tequila.

He looked down at me and smiled, but made no attempt to move. He was tall, probably a good eight inches taller than my 5'6 frame. His shoulders were broad and his dark green polo pulled slightly to contain his girth. His shirt fit his athletic frame as if it was made for him, and his jeans hung low on his narrow waist.

"Your voice is beautiful." His voice was deep and he spoke to me in low controlled words, even though we were standing so close, surrounded by what I assumed were his friends.

"Thank you. So are you." *Holy shit, did I just say that out loud?* I was glad that we were outside so that he couldn't see my face turn red; I blushed so deeply that not even my tan skin could conceal my embarrassment. I'd been thinking it, but I hadn't meant to say it. Another dangerous side effect of the tequila shots.

He smiled and raised his eyebrows in surprise. I turned my back to him to catch my breath. Tyler took it as an opportunity to offer to buy me a drink. Just as I opened my mouth to respond, the green-eyed man responded for me. "No thanks, I've got her next round." I watched in shock as his friend took the hint and walked away smiling.

I whipped around and looked up at him, a bit unsteady on my feet from the tequila. He still hadn't moved and was standing in my personal space. It was almost a possessive stance, the way he hovered above me and made his size known. "What if I wanted him to buy me a drink?"

"You don't," he said in a low voice and straight face. Was he joking or being serious?

"How do you know what I want?" I could feel the tension between us rising.

Sienna walked over, oblivious, and interrupted our little heated exchange. She was still giddy from our singing and her smile and happiness brought back such great memories. "What are you two chatting about all quietly over here?" She hung one arm around my neck and I was pretty sure she was using me to maintain her balance.

"I was just telling your friend how beautiful her voice is." He spoke to Sienna but his eyes never left me.

Sienna smiled. "Flattery will get you everywhere." She extended her hand. "I'm Sienna."

The green-eyed god took her hand in his and held it; I was relieved that his focus had finally left me. "Jack. Nice to meet you, Sienna." He quickly turned his eyes back to me. "And you are...?"

Sienna quickly intervened, slightly slurring as she spoke. "Her name is Jill." I looked up at her like she was crazy and then she winked at me. She made no attempt to hide her blatant lie and I wasn't quite sure if it was because she was drunk or if she was playing a game. I knew she was trying to subtly remind me of our earlier conversation at dinner, encouraging me to have a nameless, unattached fling. Of course, Sienna might have been trying to be subtle, but her lack of experience at subtlety made her words and actions come across as glaringly direct.

"Jill, huh?" Jack looked at me suspiciously.

I smiled. "I guess so, Jack."

"What brings you to Honolulu, Jill?" he asked with an emphasis on Jill, knowing full well it wasn't really my name.

"Well, I'm on my honeymoon, Jack!" I thought my answer was hysterical in my drunken state. Sienna must have too, considering she spit her drink out and almost choked on it, as she joined me in laughing at my statement.

For a split second, I thought Jack might have looked angry, but then he must have realized that we were teasing. Even though Sienna and I laughed our asses off, Jack didn't seem to find our joke as funny as we did. When we finally regained control of our giggling, Sienna looked up at Jack, who was clearly waiting for an explanation, smiled, then turned and went back to Jack's friends.

I looked up at Jack and he was watching me; his face showed signs of his patience slipping. "It was supposed to be my honeymoon, but we broke up two months ago. The honeymoon was already paid for, so I decided to take Sienna and make it a vacation instead."

Jack smiled, apparently content with my answer. He reached forward to the bar to grab two bottles of water. His fingers brushed mine as he handed me one, sending an electric jolt that made me pull my hand back. I looked up at him, confused.

He leaned down to my eye level and looked me straight in the eyes, briefly searching for something. "I felt it too."

A few hours later we were in the resort's bar partying with the bachelor party and had made some new friends. The bachelor, Robert, turned out to be a nice guy, who apparently was totally whipped by his fiancé. He spent most of the night getting teased and harassed by his friends, most of whom were all still single. Jack played host to the rowdy crowd and most of the staff seemed to know him by name already.

Sienna was getting cozy with Tyler as the last of the bachelor party said goodnight, leaving just the four of us. The bartender told us he was getting ready to leave and asked Jack if he wanted the keys to lock up later. "Do you work here or something?" I asked, confused, as he accepted the keys.

"Or something." Jack smiled, but offered no more information. He walked around to the other side of the bar and reached down, pulling out a bottle of water. "Drink," was all he said as he handed it to me.

"You're pretty bossy, aren't you?" I knew he was right. I needed to drink water or I would regret it the next day, but he hadn't offered it to me, he'd instructed me to drink it.

"Yes." He looked me directly in the eyes unapologetically and didn't waver the entire time he opened his own bottle and drank from it.

His stare made me dizzy, but I wasn't going to back down. The arrogant ass was starting to affect me, and it was an odd combination of being pissed off and turned on at the same time. I held his stare as I opened my water bottle and drank from it. Jack finally broke our heated gaze, and for a split second I thought I had won our unspoken challenge. Then I watched him as he slowly looked me up and down, his eyes taking their time as they wandered over my breasts and down my flat stomach. When he was done and had taken himself a good long look, his eyes returned to mine again. He didn't try to hide his visual assault; instead, he enjoyed me watching him do it. I felt a throb between my thighs and shifted my legs in response to it. He caught my body respond to him and gave me a sexy wicked smile with one eyebrow arched.

"Shit, I need to go to bed." I needed to get away from the mesmerizing man quickly before I did something stupid.

His wicked smile grew, but he didn't respond.

"Sienna, I'm going to go to bed. You coming?" I yelled to the other end of the bar where she was snuggled with Tyler.

"I'll meet you up there in a little bit, Syd."

Jack came around the bar and put his hand on the small of my back. I had to struggle to keep still, as his hand ignited my skin beneath his touch. "I'll walk you to your room." Jack tossed Tyler the keys. His hand never left me as we walked and I wondered if he felt my skin burning underneath his big hand.

"So, Syd, or is it Jill, why did Sienna not want to tell me your real name?"

Alcohol was like truth serum to me. Insert a few shots and out comes everything you ever wanted to know. "She had a crazy idea that I should have an

BELONG TO YOU

anonymous fling while we are here to celebrate my newly found singleness."

"And why is that crazy?" His tone was flat and serious.

I actually thought about the question for a minute, and couldn't come up with an answer. "Umm, I'm not sure, I guess it isn't really that crazy. People do it all the time with one night stands."

He didn't say anything more as we entered the elevator. He stood close behind me, even though there was no one else in the car. I felt his warm breath on my neck and my body was sizzling from how close he was. He had to feel it too.

Stepping off the elevator to my floor, I was disappointed to lose his body next to mine. His hand returned to the small of my back as we made our way to the door of my room. "So it's all settled then."

I was digging into my bag to find my key and looked up at him, confused, sure I must have dazed out and missed some of our conversation. He continued, "I already know your name and know you have a great voice, so it can't be total anonymity. How about if we limit each other to ten personal questions? That way we don't get to know each other that well, and it will still be sort of anonymous."

My mouth dropped open at his suggestion. I wasn't pretending to be shocked, I was shocked. "Are you saying you want to have sex with me this week and only get to ask and be asked ten personal questions?"

"That's what I'm saying." His response was dead serious.

"You're crazy." I glared at him, my face confirming that I thought he was insane.

"I thought we just established that it wasn't crazy."

"I didn't say *it* was crazy, I said *you're* crazy."

But Jack didn't respond to my accusation with words. Instead, he reached down and lifted me up effortlessly, pinning me against the door to my room, wrapping my legs around his waist. His mouth aggressively covered mine and he licked my lips, demanding them to open. Unconsciously, my lips parted and our tongues instantly collided in desperation. It wasn't a first kiss. It was *the* first kiss. We held each other tight and his mouth devoured mine harshly with a raw need raging between us. His body pressed tightly against mine and every ounce of my body was electrified from head to toe. I felt his erection hard against my stomach and knew his body was as in tune to mine as mine was to his.

He broke the kiss and leaned his forehead against mine, looking into my eyes. We were both breathless and panting. "I felt it the first minute I looked at you. You felt it too."

I couldn't deny that he was right. "Yes." The word came out breathless and throaty. It didn't even sound like my voice.

"You better unlock that door and deadbolt it quickly, before I stop being a gentleman and fuck you tonight even though you are drunk."

I bit my bottom lip and he slowly lowered me to my feet, our bodies pressed against each other intimately as I slid down from his waist.

He kissed me on the lips hard and pulled back to look at me. His beautiful green eyes turned almost gray with intensity. "No drinking tomorrow." It was more of an order than a request.

I opened the door to my room and turned back to him as he stood in the doorway. I could tell that he was fighting hard to control himself.

"Okay." I whispered and then shut the door.

Chapter 3

I woke the next morning to a knock at the door and was quickly reminded of the night before as I attempted to lift my head. My head was throbbing and I felt as though I had gone three rounds in a heavyweight match, with me being the loser of the bout. I looked over at Sienna's bed, where she was still sleeping soundly.

I answered the door to find room service with a cart. "Good morning, Ms. Aldridge, we have your breakfast ready." The waiter's voice wasn't particularly loud, yet every word felt like a nail being pushed further into my brain.

"I'm sorry, there must be a mistake, I didn't order any breakfast."

"Mr. Cole requested that we deliver to your room promptly at 11am."

"Mr. Cole?" I must have looked as confused as I was.

"He wrote a note. Maybe this will explain things." The waiter patiently stood waiting for my eyes to focus enough to take in the words on the page.

I opened the sealed hotel envelope and read the note. The handwriting was dark, neat and heavily slanted. *Good morning Jill. Drink the tomato juice; it will help with the hangover. Take two of the pills too. Eat the eggs, you will need the energy later. The flowers made me think of you. Jack.* I smiled and shook my head and directed the waiter to roll in the cart. There were two meals and an assortment of drinks, so at least he was thoughtful enough to feed us both. There was also a bottle of unopened aspirin and a beautiful arrangement of the most brightly colored wildflowers I'd ever seen.

I showed the waiter out and took a sip of the tomato juice with two aspirin. The man truly pissed me off and turned me on at the same time. It was very sweet to send me breakfast, but the note was more like an order to eat then a suggestion.

Sienna groaned as she rolled over. "You ordered me breakfast? It better be at least noon if you are waking me up." Her voice was raspy and her voice sounded like I felt.

"I didn't order it, Jack sent it. Along with instructions to eat it." The sarcasm dripped from my voice on the second sentence.

"Jack? Oh. Mmmmm. That man is delicious. You are lucky that I am a good friend who knows you need a rebound fuck, or I would have tied you up in the back of the bar to get first crack at that one." Sienna got up and went to the bathroom and then started picking at some of the food on the cart. "Let's be realistic, that man would have found you anywhere I hid you. The way he looked at you made *me* wet!"

I threw a pillow at her. "You are insane ... what doesn't make you horny, woman?" We both laughed and then devoured everything on the cart.

By the time we made our way down to the beach the sun was scorching hot. My headache subsided as I swam in the crystal clear water and reveled in the feel of the soft sand between my toes. I relished the feeling of the sun drying each droplet of water as I relaxed into my lounge chair listening to the ocean waves lightly crashing on to the shore. The rhythm of the surf eventually lulled me to sleep as I lay on my stomach listening to the tranquil sound.

I moaned as I woke to the luxurious feel of the big hands massaging my back. I was groggy and it felt so good. My muscles relaxed under the pressure of the skilled fingers. My sleepy haze drifted, reality seeped into my fantasy, and I jumped as I realized that I was at the beach and had no idea who was touching me. Jack's strong hands gently but firmly held me down on my stomach in the cushioned lounge chair as I attempted to jump up. His words were low, but there was no mistaking his sexy voice. "Don't get up, Jill, I untied your top to rub in the sunscreen and you'll give the whole beach a good show."

"You scared the shit out of me! Do you make a habit of rubbing down strangers as they sleep?"

He leaned down close to my ear, his front pressed firmly against my back. His voice was low and velvety. "Do you really want to waste one of your ten questions on my habits for rubbing down strangers?"

Shit. Though I didn't want to be, I was instantly aroused. His voice, his confident words, and his bare chest pressed up against my back, sent my body into a frenzy. My heart rate sped up and my breathing became more labored. *God damn it, control yourself, Sydney.* "You scared me half to death." I was hoping that he would believe that my reaction was from being scared and not to being near him.

"I'm sorry, baby." His voice sounded sincere and I was surprised that the man apologized for anything. "Now, if you want, I'll tie that string you call a top back on and you can get up, or we can both take a few more minutes to enjoy me rubbing your back some more."

I didn't want his hands off of me. I sighed, pretending it was a sacrifice. "Keep rubbing."

I heard a devious chuckle before he sat back up and continued to rub my back until I was completely relaxed again. Then he tied my top back on so that I could sit up.

I righted myself in the oversized lounger and caught the first glimpse of him of the day. I had a picture of him in my head as he was rubbing me, but the picture didn't come close to the real thing. His shirtless body was even more delectable than I imagined. He had strong, square shoulders, toned pecs and a six pack, which I thought only really existed in air-brushed magazines. His dark plaid swimsuit hung low on his waist, revealing a deep v that pointed to what I imagined was probably also perfect down below. Jack stood and held out his hand to help me up.

I stood and he smiled a sexy devilish grin. "My turn." He slowly looked me up and down, taking his time to admire all my girl parts. He leaned down to my ear. "Even better than I fantasized, baby."

I laughed and then went up on my tippy toes to whisper back in his ear. "You took the words right out of my mouth."

He growled, literally growled at me. Then he scooped me up and started walking toward the water.

"I can walk you know." I pretended to be annoyed, but did a lousy job since I was smiling the whole time.

"I know you can, but I'm going to take care of you the way a woman like you deserves to be taken care of this week baby."

I think my heart skipped a beat for a minute at his words. Or maybe it just started beating again finally.

I leaned back in my lounge chair and took a deep, cleansing breath, enjoying the moment. Jack was sitting up behind me, my back to his front, his hands clasped tightly around my waist in a possessive hold. We listened to the waves crash against the surf and watched the sun setting through an amazing bright orange and purple sky. It was the most beautiful sunset that I had ever seen and it felt so natural to be sitting in Jack's arms watching it.

"Why did you call off your engagement?"

"Are you cashing in on question number one, Jack?" I dared him.

"Yes, so let's hear it. And remember, I'm using one of my precious chips here, so I want the full story."

I hadn't really told many people the full story; it was still difficult to put into words. The people who really knew me just knew I was making the right decision. I wasn't sure where to start, so I decided to start from the beginning. "I met Michael in high school. We went to the prom together. We were together for six years when he proposed. I said yes, and we planned a long engagement before the wedding." I paused, contemplating before I continued.

"I don't think I ever considered not marrying him, it was just the normal progression in our long relationship and everyone expected it would happen. He would have preferred a shorter engagement, but I wasn't ready yet so I dragged it out as long as I could get away with it. He treated me really well over the years — at least I thought he did. He was every parent's dream for their daughter. He came from a good home, earned a good living as an attorney, and had nice manners. He seemed like every girl's dream too. But as the wedding got closer, I grew more nervous. I started to wonder if I had made myself into who he wanted me to be instead of who I really was. I started picturing myself having 2.5 children with a white picket fence and lunches with PTA moms who wore sweater sets.

"In the time we had been together, I had stopped singing with a band and went to school to get a music degree to teach. As my wedding date got closer, I was starting to question myself on why I had done that, when I really loved being in my band. Michael and Sienna didn't get along, and he didn't like me traveling at night to different clubs, so I eventually gave it up, even though he never actually asked me to.

"One morning I woke up having a panic attack. I realized that something was missing in our relationship and that something was me. So I sat down one night to talk to Michael about what I was feeling and he completely flipped out. He blamed it all on my last visit to NY to visit Sienna and her filling my head with crazy unrealistic singing dreams. But the truth was, Sienna never said a word to me. She accepted me for whoever I was and didn't try to change me.

"I told him that I didn't want to teach and wanted to join a local band again. He told me that his wife was not going to be a stupid band slut traveling around town with a bunch of men. We argued back and forth and then things got really heated when he realized that I had already made up my mind. The next day I felt badly about the way that we had left off, so I went to his office to talk to him and walked in on his secretary on her knees." I stopped and thought for a moment and Jack tightened his grip around me.

"I left and he tried to apologize again the next day. Eventually, when I wouldn't accept his apology, he got mad again and spilled that he had been sleeping with his secretary for more than a year anyway. I moved all of his stuff to the front lawn by the time he came home from work that night, and had the locks changed." I paused and regrouped from telling my sad tale. I forced a happier voice. "Everything happens for a reason. I quit my job teaching and started singing again last month. It's just a job as a house singer at one of the Heston Hotels, but it's a start on my trip back to me."

Jack was quiet and didn't say anything for a moment. "You work at one of the Heston Hotels?"

I laughed, thinking it was odd that of everything that I had just told him, that was the part of my story that caught his attention. Men. "Is that really a question that you want to use your second chip on?"

"Definitely."

"Yes, I work at Heston Hotel in New York City. That's how I was able to afford this fancy schmancy Heston Resort. They give a great employee discount. I moved to New York from Boston last month. I'm starting all over and doing what is right for me for a change. I'm going to start singing with Sienna again once in a while too, now that I am back in the same city again."

Quiet again. I turned to look at him and his face was unreadable. He looked into my eyes and gently brushed the hair on my face back. Then he kissed me. A different kiss from last night, not a passionate, groping kiss, but a beautiful tender kiss. It took my breath away. I couldn't remember the last time a kiss stirred so much inside of me. He watched me intently as I recovered from the moment. "Room service or Restaurant?"

I smiled at him. I wanted more than anything to say room service, but I was enjoying making him work for it a little bit. "Restaurant."

He looked at me seriously. "Whatever you want, babe. But wear a dress and forget the underwear. I want to know that it won't take me long to bury myself deep inside you after dinner."

I probably should have been offended by his crudeness, but instead it turned me on. Two could play his game. "I'd like to use my first question."

He arched one eyebrow in response, intrigued.

I volleyed his serve. "Do you prefer to be on the top or the bottom?"

His response was fast and dead serious. "I prefer whatever makes you yell louder when I fuck you harder than you've ever been fucked."

I gasped at the instant visual that his words inspired in my head. Damn, I needed a cold shower.

He stood and held out his hand to help me up. He didn't let go when I stood; instead he pulled me hard against his chest and looked down into my eyes. "And

I'm going to have you both ways tonight anyway." He smiled an evil victorious smile and grabbed my hand and started to walk into the resort.

Chapter 4

I drank a glass of wine as I got ready in my room for dinner. I was glad that Jack had said he had to take care of some business before dinner, because I needed time to pull my thoughts together. Sienna had made plans to have dinner with Tyler and we were singing at the top of our lungs as we blasted music from my iPod. I truly missed those moments, where we were both happy and singing and dancing. I didn't even realize how long it had been since I'd felt so carefree.

I picked out a pale blue strapless dress that hugged my curves in all the right places. It was the dress I knew looked good on me and always brought me compliments. My legs looked long and lean under the short skirt and the pale blue showed off my dark tan. Last time I wore it, Michael had told me that the pale blue color in the dress matched my eyes perfectly. I left my long hair down, framing my tan face. The dress made me feel pretty and gave me confidence. Oddly, I wasn't feeling as nervous as I had expected for my dinner date, and, more specifically, what was to come after dinner.

I was feeling good, and closed my eyes as I lost myself singing along with one of my favorite songs, when I turned and saw Jack standing in the doorframe. He took up most of the doorway and looked freaking amazing.

His voice was low and husky. "I was enjoying the show."

"How long were you standing there?"

"Sienna opened the door for me on her way out. You look fucking incredible."

I shook my head at his compliment and smiled, pretending I found his words harsh. "You have such a way with words." They may not have been the most eloquent, but I felt them somewhere deep inside of me. His words were raw and honest.

My comment didn't faze him in the slightest. "If I take one step into this room, I won't get to enjoy that dress and we definitely won't be going to a restaurant. So let's go before I eat you for dinner."

Even though he said it in jest, I knew he wasn't really kidding. I grabbed my bag and went quickly to the door. I opened my bag to put my room key in and a dozen condoms that must have been crammed in came popping out.

"I am going to kill Sienna." I was completely flustered and embarrassed.

"I'm going to thank her." Jack smiled a full smile and took my hand to lead me to dinner.

I was a little nervous that dinner would be awkward because we both knew what was going to happen afterward. But it was just the opposite. Our conversation flowed so freely it was hard to believe that we had only met the day before. We talked and teased and laughed all the way through dinner and drinks. He ordered us a dessert I had never heard of with two spoons and I noticed that the waiter and most of the staff all seemed to know him by name.

"Do you come here often? Everyone seems to know your name."

"Question number two. Yes, I come here a few times a year. It's one of my favorite hotels."

I pouted. "That isn't really a personal question. I don't think I should get charged for that one!"

"Asking a person where they vacation qualifies as a personal question."

"Fine. But I want it noted that I used that one under protest."

He pretended to be serious, but I saw the corners of his glorious mouth twitch upwards. "So noted." A pause, and then, "My turn. Are you on birth control?"

"Question number three. You are going to cash in all of your chips before the end of the game, if you aren't careful."

Both his eyebrows arched in surprise and he smirked, but waited for my answer.

"Yes, I'm on birth control and I just had a physical last month. I'm clean. I thought I might save you a question and throw in the second part for free." I arched one eyebrow and smirked back at him. "My turn. When—" I started but was quickly interrupted by Jack.

"Save the question, I'll donate the answer. Physical. Three week ago. Clean as a whistle. Plus, I've always used a condom."

"Always?" I assumed he was exaggerating.

His face was serious. "That one's gonna cost you. Question number three. Every. Single. Time."

I was intrigued and starting to get turned on. It wasn't typical first date conversation, but yet it seemed oddly normal to be talking about it with him. "And you want your first time without one to be with me?"

"Question number four. More than I've ever wanted anything." He ran his fingers through his sexy hair. Jack had the type of hair that looked like he'd just had sex and I was more than a little jealous that it was his fingers delving into his hair and not mine. But I was glad to see that he had a tell, the first sign that our conversation was starting to affect him too. He caught my eye and said, "I want to feel every bit of you. Then I want to pump myself into you so far that you can feel it seep deep into your body."

Oh. My. God. I had to recross my legs and clamp my thighs tightly together to keep my body from responding to just his words.

"Are you wearing underwear?" His voice was low and raspy. I heard the desire pour from his words.

"Question number four." I bit my lip and hesitated for a brief second. "No." I had barely finished my word when Jack lifted me up and out of my seat and grabbed my hand, heading for the door. We flew by the waiter bringing out our dessert.

"Put it on my room, Eduardo," he yelled to the poor confused waiter without slowing down. I had to practically run behind him just to keep up.

We weaved through the hotel hallways, arrived at the elevator, and neither of us said a word as we got in, finding an older couple already occupying the car. Jack stood close behind me and inserted a room key into the control panel, wrapping his arms tightly around my waist as the car began to travel.

I could feel my heart beating out of my chest and I was certain that the couple next to us could too. The car stopped to let out the couple and the tension grew as the doors closed, leaving us alone in the car. Jack pushed a button on the panel and I felt his mouth on my neck from behind me. His wet full lips kissed and sucked at the tender spot between my neck and shoulder. A small moan escaped my lips and he responded by pressing me against the mirrored car wall. The palms of my hands were spread wide against the cold hard mirror, my face turned to the side, the cold not helping to reduce the heat in my body. He kissed my neck, tracing his tongue up from my collarbone to my ear. I could feel his arousal as he pushed gruffly into my back, pinning me between his hold and the wall.

His hands reached down to the outside of my thighs, burning a trail of heat as they felt their way slowly around to my bare ass. I gasped as he lifted my skirt and pushed his hard body deeper into my bare back. I was desperate to feel him against me, skin against skin. He bit my ear and I stopped breathing, anticipating his traveling hands as they reached around me and slowly moved down from my belly button, finally reaching my swollen clit.

His hand cupped me. "You're so wet for me," he growled in my ear. His voice couldn't hide his lack of control. Two of his large fingers pressed my clit and began massaging in small circles. I almost orgasmed at just his first touch.

"Is everything okay in the car? It looks like you have been stopped between floors." The voice from the control panel hit me lack a bucket of ice water thrown on my face, bringing me back to reality.

"Fuck," Jack groaned, and rested his forehead on the mirror above my head. He took a loud deep breath and pushed a button on the panel to respond. "We're fine." His answer was sharp and swift. He pulled the hem of my dress down and inserted the key into the panel again. As the car began traveling, he repositioned himself behind me, and we both quietly faced the front of the car.

"I'm sorry, you deserve better than that." His voice was tense and low.

"Don't be, I enjoyed it." My answer was honest and came out between heavy breaths. He turned me and looked into my eyes, searching my face for confirmation. I smiled and arched an eyebrow and was rewarded with a smile and laugh. He lowered his head and kissed me firmly on my lips before taking my hand and leading us out of the elevator.

We arrived at a door and he opened it, leading me inside. The suite was beautiful, and five times the size of my room, but I noticed it wasn't the penthouse. "I thought you and your friends were all staying together in the penthouse?"

"We were. I moved to this room today so we would have privacy." He made no attempt to hide his assumption.

"Pretty sure of yourself, aren't you?" I teased as I walked to the glass wall leading to a large open balcony.

He opened the door for me to go outside. "I knew what I wanted the minute I saw your face. I'm a man that gets what he wants, one way or another. I'll give you that personal information for free."

I laughed at his answer, but somehow I knew his words were true. Jack was a man who knew what he wanted and got it. I looked out at the ocean. The view was breathtaking from the balcony and I could hear the ocean singing in the not too far distance. I took a deep breath and smelled the salt air mixed with flowers. I closed my eyes as I leaned against the railing, enjoying the sounds and the smell of the ocean air. Jack stood behind me. He placed one hand on each side of the railing around me and we stayed that way for long moments in silence.

"Are you close with your family?" I felt his body tense and I immediately regretted asking the question. A long moment of silence passed before he answered my question.

"Question number five. I don't speak to my father and my mom passed away last year."

"I'm so sorry." I didn't know what else to say.

"Thank you." A long pause and then I was surprised when he continued. "When I was eighteen, my dad gave me a portion of my inheritance from my grandfather to see if I could manage money before releasing the balance of my trust fund to me. The trust fund gave my dad the authority to release the funds to me at any time after my eighteenth birthday, if he thought that I was capable of managing the responsibility. If he didn't think I was responsible enough, I wasn't to gain access until my twenty-fifth birthday. Two weeks after my birthday I caught him with a prostitute in his office. My mom had just been diagnosed with cancer and the asshole was so selfish that he couldn't keep it in his pants to take care of his sick wife. He knew I wouldn't hurt my mom in her condition by telling her, so he took advantage. After that, I caught him with at least three more prostitutes before I stopped speaking to him altogether, except when we were in front of my mother. The bastard made me keep his secrets for seven years while my mother underwent six rounds of chemotherapy and four different surgeries."

I wasn't sure how to respond, but I was curious. My big mouth had taken us from bliss to bad memories in a span of fifteen minutes. "Did you have to wait until you were twenty-five for your trust fund?"

He laughed. "Question number six. I partied for the first year and wasted a shitload of money. Then my father, being the upstanding pillar of the community that he thought he was, decided to run for senate. Apparently having 40,000 employees didn't give him enough power, he needed to conquer the world." Jack walked to a table between the lounge chair that had a bottle of wine chilling and two glasses.

"So, I invested the money I had left into a business that I knew would embarrass him and hurt his chances of winning a campaign based on his pretend Christian morals." He handed me a glass of wine and I watched as he tilted his own glass back and swallowed his wine in one large gulp. "The funny thing is, I didn't need the trust fund after that. My business investment turned out to be very successful. But the bastard released the balance of the trust fund to me the same day that he withdrew from the senate race. I'm sure he was trying to send me a message that I had ruined his race, but I saw it as the last tear in the cloth that kept us bound together."

Wow. Jack had shared so much information about who he was and his life in only a few minutes, I wasn't sure what to do with it. But it stirred something inside of me that this beautiful man was so honest with me about the hurt caused by his father. I turned to face him. His arms never left the railing, blocking me in. He watched intently as I brought my wine glass to my lips and tipped my head back to empty it, mimicking his actions from a few minutes ago.

He took my glass and placed it down. Then he reached down and lifted me up and cradled me in his arms as he walked back inside where he gently laid me on the bed. I watched as he walked to the foot of the bed and slowly removed each of my sandals. His eyes never left mine.

He trailed kisses along the arch of my foot, traveling up the inside of my calf. I was instantly reduced to a quivering mess of anticipation. He worked his tongue with skill over every part of my legs, gently alternating between nipping and sucking as he burned a path up my body. When he reached between my legs, he paused, taking his time to look at my most intimate area that was bared to him. His armed wrapped around my lower back and he raised my pelvis so that I had a clear line of vision to watch him. Every part of my body was on high alert, sensitive to every movement and desperate for more of his touch.

He ran his tongue up and down my sex gently at first, then found my clit with a strong suck that drove me wild. My hands dug into his hair and I moaned without self-control. He responded to my sound ferociously, releasing my clit and plunging his tongue inside of me deeply.

"Shit," I groaned. I was going to cum from only thirty seconds of his mouth on me. I was close to the edge as he continued to plow his tongue in and out of me. He returned to my clit and sucked while swirling his tongue around in small counterclockwise circles. I felt his hand move from my thigh and two of his large fingers slipped easily inside my wetness. He pumped twice and I went flying over the edge in the most intense orgasm of my life. I had never had an orgasm outside of the plain old missionary position.

I opened my eyes and looked down at him, my fingers still wrapped tightly in his dark brown hair. His eyes were on me and I felt slightly exposed coming down from my rollercoaster orgasm. "That was the most beautiful thing I've ever seen in my life." His voice was raspy and his warm breath on my clit made my body tingle.

I gave a small smile, feeling slightly embarrassed and vulnerable at the intensity at which his words were spoken.

"Something that beautiful needs to be seen often," he said before giving my clit one last twirl with his expert tongue. He slowly pulled himself up over my body, his tongue tasting me as he traveled upward. He reached my nipple and swirled it around gently until it was swollen and protruding. Then he bit down hard, sending a jolt of electricity down to my already swollen clit, a pleasurable feeling coming from somewhere on the border of pain.

When I was panting loudly, he pulled me up to a sitting position and lifted my dress over my head, tossing it carelessly on the floor. He pulled his shirt over his head and revealed the rippled body that I had been pleasantly introduced to on the beach earlier. He raised himself to his knees between my open legs and tugged his pants down, revealing he was not wearing underwear either. It was the first time I got a glimpse of him naked, in all his glory. His cock was tremendous and stood firmly at attention, reaching all the way up to his belly button. My eyes trailed back up to his face and again I found him watching me as I looked him over.

"If you keep looking at me like that, you may get locked in this room for a week." His lips devoured mine in a possessive assault and I was breathless when he broke the kiss. He guided me back down to the bed, hovering over me as my body took his weight. At that moment, I couldn't think of anything in the world except how badly I wanted him inside of me.

He grasped both of my hands and held them firmly above my head with one of his large hands. His other hand gently caressed my face. I was at his mercy and loved every minute of it. He watched me intently as he positioned himself and then slowly he tilted his hips and entered me halfway.

He growled. "You're so tight, you okay?"

I shook my head, unable to form words. He rocked his hips back and forth a few times to open my tunnel, always keeping his eyes locked to mine. When I relaxed and a low moan rose from my throat, I watched as his face changed and he began to lose his control. I pulled one of my hands free from his grip and dug my nails into his back as I pulled him closer to me, wanting him to give me more. He couldn't hold back anymore either. His lips pummeled mine and his tongue invaded my mouth as he slammed his full length into me. He was buried deep inside of me and I was teetering on a fine line between pleasure and pain.

He rocked into me over and over, his heavy balls slapping into my ass. When my body sufficiently loosened to accommodate his wide girth, I tilted my hips up to give him more access. Two more thrusts and I rode over the edge again in a blissful orgasm. I moaned through the ferocious waves of pleasure and it was his undoing. He growled as he thrust into me a few last times, before emptying himself into me.

He took a harsh breath and released my hand from his death grip above my head. "Fuck, Syd, I have no self control around you. Sex is usually only a release of energy for me — when it's over, I'm done — but every time I touch you I only want you more." His gaze was serious.

Yet again I should probably have been insulted at his words. I may not have had many partners, but I knew enough to know that pillow talk about your sex life with other people was a big fat no-no. But for some reason, his words warmed me. "And I just had my first orgasm without intercourse, so I guess we both might be addicted now." I smiled and blushed at my own words.

Jack raised both his eyebrows in surprise and smiled down at me, shaking his head in amusement.

We stayed in bed the rest of the night, holding each other, our legs still tangled when we awoke the next morning. I raised my eyes to look at him and was surprised to find him awake and watching me. "Good morning, sleepyhead." He gently stroked my hair as he spoke.

"Good morning. How long have you been awake?"

"A few hours."

I rose and looked at him in disbelief. "A few hours, what time did you get up?"

"Six."

"Do you always get up that early?" Looking down at him, my face told him that I found it insane that anyone would get up that early when they didn't have to.

"Question number seven." He smiled. "Yes. I'm up and out for a run by 5am usually. You should be grateful that I didn't wake you and demand you go with me for a quick ten miles."

"I'm not sure what is more disturbing to me in that

answer, the fact that you think a ten mile run is quick or that you think you could demand I go with you."

He grinned and looked at me like I had just offered him a challenge. "There are a lot of things that I plan to demand from you, babe. And you're going to do them all for me."

"Is that so?" I did my best to sound insulted, but the truth was that I was excited at the thought of him demanding anything from me inside the bedroom.

He flipped me onto my back and kissed me passionately. His tongue stroked the inside of my mouth and I bit his bottom lip fiercely. Within a minute, we were both panting and I tried to wrap my legs around his waist to tempt him into giving me more, but he flipped us over and suddenly I was on top.

The way he looked at me made me feel sexy and uninhibited as I sat up, straddling him on both sides of his muscled thighs. I lifted up to allow his thick cock the space it needed to enter me and then I hovered over him, his wide head sitting at my entrance. He grabbed my waist and held me in place, looking in my eyes. "Slow," he commanded.

I held his eyes the entire time I slowly lowered myself down the entire length of his large shaft. I circled my hips, taking him all in, and allowed my eyes to close and my head to drop back as he filled me completely.

"Fuck, Syd," he said through clenched teeth. "I'm going to cum. I can't watch you and hold back when you look like that."

His words excited me. I became so wet that I easily slid up and down his cock as I began to ride him. My pace quickened as I felt my own orgasm build, and he gripped my waist to take control of my movements. He needed me to go slow to maintain control, and I need to go faster to lose mine. I ground down on him as hard as I could, desperate to get the friction I needed.

"Slow." He growled again in an authoritative voice that was desperate to regain the control. One hand released my hip and found my clit, giving me what I needed as he pushed me over the edge. I slowed and let it take over me as it pulsed through my body. "Look at me." Jack held my eyes locked to his and watched as the orgasm ripped through me. I would normally close my eyes, but the way he looked at me with such possessive need made me cum harder than I ever had in my life.

"Fuck," he roared as he thrust his hips up, his arms back at my waist controlling my thrusts in time to meet his with each hard pound down. I wanted to watch his orgasm rip through him, almost as much as I needed mine to take over me. His already tight body went rock hard as he pumped twice more and came inside of me with a growl.

I collapsed on top of him and he stroked my damp hair as we both struggled to regain our breath. "You do things to me, Syd," he said quietly.

I smiled. Such an easy one. "I like to do things to you."

We both laughed and eventually he dragged me out of bed and into the shower.

"I better call Sienna so she doesn't worry." I was dressed in only a towel after our shower.

"She isn't worried; she is expecting us in half an hour." He handed me a Heston Hotels t-shirt and shorts. I looked at him, confused, but he didn't seem to notice. "The hotel shops aren't open yet and it was all I could get the concierge to find this morning."

"Thank you." I slipped the t-shirt on over my head and let the towel drop to the floor. "Why is Sienna expecting us?"

"I made plans with Tyler. We are taking you ladies to the other side of the island for surfing lessons."

I squealed with excitement and jumped up and down. His mouth twitched and he laughed.

The bathroom in the suite was heavily stocked with some of the essentials I was missing, moisturizer, a toothbrush and a blow dryer. I did my morning routine as best as I could and blow dried my long hair. When I came out fifteen minutes later, Jack had a full breakfast delivered. "Hungry?"

I smiled. "Question number five. Starving."

"That does not count as a personal question, babe. A personal question is how many partners have you had or how old were you when you lost your virginity."

"Okay then. Question number five. One, actually two now. And sixteen."

"That shouldn't count either, I wasn't asking the

question … wait, what, did you say one?" His head snapped to look at me as I sipped my juice.

"Yep, you are number two." I could tell by his face that he was shocked at my answer. His reaction made me curious enough to cash in a question. "And how many partners have you had, Jack?"

"Is that question number eight?"

I nodded.

"More than two?" His response was a question, as if to ask if that was going to be an acceptable answer.

"I'm going to need a little more specific of an answer." I smiled and waited, letting him squirm for a while. Even though I had only been with one man, it didn't mean I was naïve. I knew that a man that looked the way he did would have ample opportunity.

"I don't have an exact count," he said after considering his response.

I found it adorable that he was afraid to give me an answer. "Ballpark, babe."

His eyes looked away from me. "Somewhere between 500 and 1,000?"

I spit my juice all over the place. Holy. Shit. I knew he was handsome and it sounded like he was wealthy, but 500 to 1000, really? That wasn't normal, was it? I made a mental note to ask Sienna about it. "That's crazy, how do you have time for anything else?" I teased.

He looked embarrassed and it made me feel badly for playing with him.

"I'm teasing. I guess I'm a lucky woman then to have

my rebound fling have such experience. I'll be expecting to learn a lot of new tricks this week, playboy."

I saw him flinch, so I jumped up into his arms, wrapping my legs around him. He wrapped his arms around my bottom to hold me in place. "You have no underwear on. If you don't want me to fuck you on the serving cart and be late to meet your friend, you'd better jump down and eat quickly."

I kissed him on the cheek and smiled, letting him know that I wasn't really upset. Then I jumped down and ate my breakfast because I was sure that Jack would make good on his word if I tempted him.

Chapter 5

The ride to the other end of the island was amazing. Jack rented an open air jeep and Sienna and I sang loudly along with most of the songs on the radio. The scenery was beautiful and we all laughed and enjoyed the ride. I found myself again thinking about how long it had been since I'd felt so carefree and happy.

We arrived at the beach and went toward the beach hut to check in for our surf lessons. The guy working looked like he had just stepped out of a surfer magazine. He had long, sun-bleached hair, a dark tan and was wearing sunglasses secured with a lanyard around his head loosely. As we approached he came around the counter, smiling.

"Jack, dude, long time no see." He clasped Jack's hand and pulled him into a one-armed guy hug.

"Bones, how are you man? It's been a while," Jack responded.

"All good, all good. Still taking it one wave at a time. I got the message you were coming down today to get some friends lessons so I had to stop down and check things out. You gonna catch some waves with me for old times' sake while your friends get their school on?"

"Sounds good, as long as you let me ride the Bone Maker."

Bones laughed and walked around the corner. "You got it, man. You know I don't let just anyone ride the Bone Maker."

"I'm touched." Jack held his hand over his heart in feigned sincerity.

"So who we got here? These two beautiful women have names, playboy?" Bones motioned in our direction.

"This is Sydney and Sienna. And the big ugly guy is Tyler." Tyler shook his head and laughed. The two men focused their attention on insulting each other, but underneath there was warmth that told their true friendship. "Where's Val? She's going to give Syd a lesson today." Jack looked around as he spoke.

"Sorry, dude, they tried to call you back, but you had already left. Val couldn't get here … she's stuck on Maui doing a photoshoot for some suntan lotion shit. She was supposed to be back this morning but, Val being Val and all, she missed her flight. But don't worry man, we hooked you up. Guy Stokes is in town for a qualifying round for the nationals and we got him to fill in for Val." Bones motioned toward the water where a surfer was walking our way carrying his board.

Holy. Shit. I thought I'd died and gone to surfer god heaven. The man coming toward us was breathtaking.

Tall, lean, and perfectly tanned with a chiseled face and long bleached hair pulled back in a loose pony tail. Definitely not the kind of man I would normally be attracted to, but that kind of man doesn't walk by all too often.

"I hope that is my instructor, hot damn," Sienna crowed, without a care in the world that the man she was currently sleeping with was standing right next to her. I looked to Tyler and he didn't seem the least bit bothered by her comment.

Bones laughed. "Sorry there, Sienna, Stokes is all for your friend today. He doesn't usually give lessons, but we had to find some big guns to fill in for Val."

"Bitch," Sienna hissed at me.

Bones and I both laughed at Sienna's response as the surfing god approached.

"Which one of you beautiful ladies is mine for the day?" Stokes flirted, giving his full attention to Sienna and I, completely ignoring Jack and Tyler.

"I raised my hand shyly. That would be me."

"Damn, I'm one lucky man." Stokes shook my hand, holding it longer than a normal handshake.

"I hope you go easy on me, it's my first time." I hadn't meant it to come out so flirty, but it did nonetheless.

"I always go easy on first timers. We'll take our time and go nice and slow." Sexuality poured out of his every word.

I'm pretty sure I blushed. Jack's deep voice snapped me out of my momentary bubble with the surfer god.

"Change of plans. You are with Sienna today." Jack moved closer and put his hand on the small of my back.

I turned and saw Jack's stone face. His expression and stance clearly left no room for debate. Jack was staking his claim on me and, oddly enough, it turned me on.

Bones shook his head and laughed. "Never thought I'd see the day, dude." He gave us all boards and Jack carried both of ours down to the water, where we all parked our stuff on two lounge chairs. I slipped out of my shorts and tank and found Jack watching me.

"You like what you see?" I whispered to him as we all changed.

Jack ran his fingers through his hair and leaned in to whisper back to me. "I want to rip that little bikini off and run my tongue from that sexy freckle on the inside of your thigh up into that sweet hole and taste your sweet cream."

Holy. Shit. Did he just really say that? I looked around to see if anyone was listening but everyone else seemed to be engrossed in conversation and oblivious to us. I felt my clit swell and my nipples harden and I was sure that everyone on the beach knew I was damp between my legs. When my eyes made their way back to Jack's, he gave me a sexy smile and arched one eyebrow, as if he were waiting for my response. He expected me to respond and I could barely breathe I was so turned on. Instead, I did the only thing that came into my mind. I reached up onto my tippy toes and pressed my body into his and kissed him hard.

It took a minute after I broke the kiss to realize that everyone who had been oblivious to us a minute ago had become silent and was watching us intently. Stokes took a deep breath and slowly looked me up and down, not hiding his seductive gaze in the slightest. "Damn, you sure you don't want me to give Syd a lesson, dude?"

Sienna jokingly punched him and Tyler laughed. Jack, apparently, did not find anything funny. He grabbed my hand and our boards and pulled me to the water with a murderous look on his face.

We spent the day in the water riding the waves and either Jack was a great teacher or I was a quick learner because I was able to stand after only a few tries. Without having to waste any of my remaining questions, I learned that Jack had patience and was a good teacher. We played in the water together and eventually wound up wrapped in each other's arms, floating in the waves. On the way back to the resort, I found my mind wandering again. When was the last time I'd felt so happy and carefree before this week? I couldn't remember. Surely, I must have felt the same type of happiness with Michael in the beginning. I just couldn't remember when things had changed. Michael and I didn't do outdoor sports together and I had forgotten how much I enjoyed the simple things like bodysurfing at the beach. For a long time I felt like that part of my life was over. Almost as if that type of fun was for kids. But I was beginning to realize that it didn't have to be that way.

Chapter 6

The minute we entered our room, Sienna began her inquisition. She must have been about ready to burst with all the questions she had stored up for me. "Holy shit, Syd, that man wouldn't let another man touch you with a ten foot pole! Normally I would think possessive was annoying, but on that man it is sexy as all hell. He's so into you. And speaking of into you, spill on the sex."

The honest truth was that I wanted to share with Sienna; I just didn't know how to do it. I had spent so much time with Michael that I never learned to dish because I didn't have flings to dish about. Sienna, on the other hand, made dishing a science. She could give a blow by blow of her night that would rival the best erotica novelist. "It was awesome." God I sucked at dishing.

"Well, I could have told you that just looking at the man!" She wasn't going to accept my three word summary of my escapades.

"I guess I just don't have much to compare it to, but if I am comparing it to sex with Michael, it's like comparing the Rolling Stones to our eighth grade band, Punk White girls." I might not be good at giving an account of my sexual promiscuity, but I could always get my point across to Sienna with a music analogy. "He's a bit dominating, but it's mixed with a hint of a sexy sweetness somewhere down deep, so it isn't overwhelming. And, it helps that he is well endowed."

After all of the years we had been friends, Sienna was a master at reading my mind through what I didn't say rather than the words I spoke. "I knew it, I knew that asshole Michael had a little prick!" We both cracked up on the bed like we were in ninth grade again.

"Just be careful, Syd. This is supposed to be your rebound fling. I don't want to see you getting hurt." It wasn't a lecture, I knew she meant well: I didn't have much experience with men, especially men like Jack, and I was just out of a bad breakup.

"I will, Sienna. He's just made me realize that I was dead for a lot of years, just going through the motions and not controlling my own life." I sighed. "I didn't know how much I needed this week."

Dinner with Tyler, Sienna and Jack was entertaining, to say the least. We laughed the entire time and I saw a new, playful side of Jack. Tyler and Jack went back as far as Sienna and I, and their history together was anything but tame. Tyler told stories of them growing up together and all of the fights they got into. Sienna and I told stories of the fights we'd caused.

After dinner Tyler asked if we wanted to go dancing at the resort's club. Jack answered before I could respond. "Another night, we have plans." Sienna looked at me and I shrugged my shoulders.

Tyler slapped Jack on the shoulder. "Whatever, man. You guys have a good night. Just remember the boys own your ass tomorrow for our trip."

I said goodnight to Sienna and Jack led us out of the restaurant with his hand burning a hole at the small of my back. "So, what plans do we have?" I smiled up at the beautiful man, intrigued at what he had planned.

He wrapped his arms around my waist, pulling me close to him. "I do have plans for us, but I'm not sure if I'll make it the next few hours without being inside of you."

I swallowed. Why did his domineering attitude turn me on, when if Michael had tried to control me I would have fled? "Well, maybe we should do something about that before we attend to your plans."

He raised his eyebrow in a challenge. "You do realize that I will fuck you right here in the hall if you keep teasing me, right?"

Although it sounded like something someone would say to make a point, I was pretty sure from the way he was looking at me that he would actually do it. I bit my lip and went to say something back to him, then decided it might not be a good idea to poke a pacing lion looking to pounce, and clamped my mouth shut.

"Fuck." He slammed his mouth into mine and I submitted to the most possessive, wildly sensual kiss I ever had in my life. I was panting and dizzy when the kiss broke. Jack grabbed my hand and I followed him as he sped down the halls, determined to get to some destination. I had to stop wearing such high heels when I was with this man, as he seemed to have a habit of leaving me breathless and dragging me off like a caveman.

Jack opened a door and we entered what must have been a hotel employee's office. From the look of it, I would have guessed that it was a manager's office. Before I could get a good look around to really see where we were, he was on me. The passion from the kiss a few minutes before only escalated. His tongue stroked mine and I could feel his heart pounding against my chest as he held me tight to him and I was acutely aware of every hard muscle pressed up against me.

"I need to fuck you fast and hard now, babe. I'll make it up to you with slow and sweet later." He was telling me, not asking for permission, although I nodded my agreement anyway.

He turned me around and pushed us to the corner of the room where the desk sat. He bent me forward and leaned my body over the desk, my arms extending forward over the length of the desk. "Hold onto the desk, babe."

I did as I was told. I was vaguely aware of him pulling up my skirt and then I felt his finger cupping my sex. "You're so fucking wet for me. God I need to be inside you." I heard his zipper go down and then his right arm reached around my waist, hoisting my ass higher up in the air and holding me firmly in place. I was bent over a desk, completely exposed and never more aroused in my life.

I felt the head of his swollen cock at my opening and then he thrust into me deeply in one long spear. My back tried to arch, but his arm held me firmly bent over in place where he needed me. My body clenched around his thickness and I thought I might come before he even had a chance to pull back out once. His hips slowly circled, and he gently pulled out an inch and pushed back in a few times. I could feel him straining to maintain his control. "You ready for me, babe?"

My body ached and my mind couldn't focus on anything but satisfying my body. "Yes." It came out as demanding and as frustrated as I felt.

Jack pulled out and slammed his thick cock into me. I cried out with ecstasy as he slammed in and out with deep, hard thrusts. My body gave in and my hips pushed back to meet every demanding deep spear. I moaned as I felt my body radiate and begin to tremble all over.

"Fuck, fuck. Come for me now," he demanded. My body acted on his command without hesitation, a full wave of orgasm ripping through me at his words. I cried out, wild for him, and let my body take him in.

He came with a ferocious growl as he pounded into me relentlessly. I felt his orgasm tear through him.

We laid panting for a minute, his chest leaning on my back. He kissed the back of my neck and my shoulder, sending tingles down my spine. He stood and the cool air hit my damp neck. My body reacted with a shiver. From behind, Jack lifted me up and cradled me, carrying me to a couch I hadn't realized was there. He laid on his back and cradled me to his chest.

"I can't get enough of you." His voice was raspy and low.

"Me too." I turned my head and kissed his hard chest before snuggling back into his arms.

We laid there for a while in comfortable silence. I had no idea where I was or who might walk in, yet it didn't bother me. Somehow I knew nothing would happen to me while I was in Jack's arms.

"As much as I'd rather take you upstairs to my room and start round two now, I'm going to take you out as I planned. I know you didn't come all this way to see the inside of my suite, so I'm going to show you some of my favorite places on the island. " He gently kissed the top of my head and I felt my heart swell a little.

We drove in the dark for almost a half hour, half of the time spent winding our way up and around a narrow road. I was glad I wasn't driving, because I was barely able see the road and I knew we were getting higher, as I felt my ears pop as we made our slow ascent. Jack pulled to the side of the road as we reached flat land. He came around and opened my door and took my hand to help me from the Jeep. He reached in the back and pulled out a blanket and laced my fingers through his, tugging me to follow.

We walked through the darkness onto a grassy field. There were no other cars in sight and we were far from streetlights and noise. Jack spread the blanket out and wrapped his arms around me, pulling me gently down to the blanket. I wasn't sure where we were or what we were doing, but I didn't care when Jack's arms were wrapped around me.

"Close your eyes."

I did as instructed and closed my eyes, although it was so dark outside that the view didn't actually change that much. Jack positioned me on my back and then I felt him lie next to me, holding my hand.

"Okay, open." I opened my eyes slowly and gasped at the sight. A million stars danced and twinkled, so close it looked as if I could reach my hand out and grab one.

"Wow, this is incredible." I stared up in awe of the lights that were dancing in the sky.

Jack held my hand and lifted my arm pointing to the sky, slowly tracing the trail between the brightest stars. "The Big Dipper." He connected the dots to seven bright stars with our joined hands. There were four shaped together to form the bowl and three to form the handle. "The Little Dipper." He connected the dots to trace the next picture, close to the first one. He pointed out all the named constellations he knew and then we took turns finding our own pictures in the sky. I found a heart and a tree; he found a dog and a bike. We lay there together, both of us on our backs, hand in hand for hours talking and drawing pictures in the sky.

"Tell me about your last girlfriend," I asked softly as we studied the sky.

"Question number nine. This one was wasted, Syd" Jack chuckled. "I was sixteen and we went out for three months. She dumped me when I got caught making out with her best friend."

I laughed; surely he was kidding, but he didn't say more. "Are you saying you haven't had a girlfriend since you were sixteen?"

"Yep."

I turned on my side, propping myself up on my elbow to look at him. "You don't expect me to believe that a gorgeous man like you, who is incredible in bed, has only had one girlfriend, when he was sixteen?"

"I'm glad you think I'm incredible in bed." His voice was so damn sexy.

"Don't try to change the subject, Jack, we agreed that we each got to ask ten questions that got ten truthful answers. You told me you had 500 to 1,000 partners?"

He took a deep breath in and exhaled loudly. "I told you the truth both times. I had one girlfriend, but lots of partners."

"So all of the others were one night stands?" I knew he had to have had lots of casual sex in order to have so many partners, but something about only having one girlfriend freaked me out a bit.

"No, Syd. Some of them were more than one night stands. But I wouldn't say that any of them were my girlfriends, other than when I was sixteen." His tone was getting stronger and more defensive.

"Define girlfriend." I thought maybe we had different definitions of the terms.

He was quiet for a minute. "Someone you see on a regular basis that you care for and have a mutually exclusive relationship with."

Okay, so I couldn't chalk his answer up to a difference in a definition. How could this gorgeous man who had just taken me to his favorite spot to show me the stars not have found someone to have a relationship with? There must have been women clamoring at the opportunity. "I can't imagine you lacked the opportunity. Is it the mutually exclusive part that you weren't interested in?"

He was quiet for a long moment. I liked that he didn't just spit out an answer for the sake of hearing himself speak, as many men would have done. He seemed to give my questions due consideration before he responded. "I enjoy sex and spending time with women. But I have my business and a life and I guess I never found anyone that made me want to complicate things."

"Complicate things?" You see having a girlfriend as a complication?" I couldn't hide the appall in my voice.

His tone changed and I could tell he was getting more defensive. "How did your relationship end? I'd call that complicated."

I rolled back on my back and took a deep breath. He was right, relationships were complicated. A week or two of fun with someone like we were doing now was probably much more simple.

Jack lifted himself and brought his face close to mine. "I'm sorry, babe, I didn't mean that to come out the way it did." He kissed me chastely on the mouth.

"It's okay. I think it only bothered me because you are probably right. I always believed in happily ever after, but maybe those endings really are only for fairytales."

"No." I jumped at his booming response, startled; his voice was stern and unexpected. "You deserve a happily ever after, don't listen to my shit." He lifted himself up and reached out his hand to help me up. My stupid questions had upset him again. Jack had given me a great day at the beach, a fun dinner with friends, and a sweet evening under the stars, and I had ruined it with more prodding.

The drive home seemed longer than the drive there. We both were quiet and our conversation was limited to discussing the radio station and Jack pointing to a few landmarks as we passed by. It was the first time since I met him that there was any uncomfortable silence.

I could hear the music blaring and people having fun at the outdoor poolside bar as we passed through the open air lobby. "Do you want to go have a drink?" I wanted to change the mood, but wasn't sure how to do it.

"I have to get up early in the morning. The guys and I are taking a day trip over to the island of Paui for an all day fishing trip. Our flight leaves at 7am." His voice was distant and my heart sank at his response. He was ending our fling. I knew what it was when it started, but we had so much fun and chemistry I had let myself get lost in it. I couldn't let him see me get upset.

"That sounds like fun." I did my best perky and carefree impression.

Jack walked me to my room and I tried to hide my disappointment. He kissed me and watched the door close before leaving. It was the first time since I met him that we didn't make any plans to see each other again. Inside my room, I didn't cry, although I was sad. Sienna had been right, I had started to have feelings for Jack and needed to be careful and see it for what it was, a rebound fling.

Chapter 7

I woke to the phone ringing the next morning. The hotel manager had heard about Sienna and I singing at the bar a few nights ago and wanted to know if we would fill in for the lead singer at the resort's nightly themed party. The band's lead singer had come down with the flu and the backup they usually used was in Maui working a wedding that night. I wasn't really in the mood to sing, but the manager's desperation made me feel guilty knowing that I could help him. Plus, technically, the hotel was my employer, and it wouldn't look good if anyone heard that I'd refused to help out with a singing gig when I was available. I reluctantly agreed and told him that we would come down and rehearse later in the afternoon with the band.

Sienna was in surprisingly good shape that morning and seemed genuinely excited about our gig when I told her about it. We decided to spend the day at the beach before our rehearsal. We both put on our bikinis, sarongs, our big floppy hats, and filled our straw bags with tabloid magazines and iPods.

The beach was quiet and we found two loungers near a straw hut. We positioned our chairs to face the sun and both tilted our chairs down to lie on our backs.

"What happened with you and Jack? I was surprised to find you in our room when I came in this morning."

"He said he had to get up early for a fishing trip to an outer island this morning." I wanted to hide the disappointed in my voice, but Sienna knew me too well.

"Oh. I didn't think that man was going to let you out from underneath him the whole week. You okay?"

"Yeah, I'm fine. I guess I just assumed it was going to last the whole week too, but I think the fling has flung and we are done." I tried my best at casual.

Sienna smiled at me. "Well, whatever it was it seemed to work. You didn't spend the first few days of our honeymoon talking about that asshole Michael at least."

She was right. I had barely even thought about Michael the last few days, unless I was comparing him to Jack and he was landing on the light side of the scale. I'm sure she had expected me to be sad and reminiscent about my years with Michael on our trip. After all, we were on the honeymoon that I had planned to spend with Michael. The odd thing was that I missed Jack more than Michael.

I smiled. "Who could think of Michael with Jack as a distraction?"

"Well, I'm glad you enjoyed yourself with him. If you're done, can I have him now?" Sienna teased.

A quiet day on the beach was just what I needed. We soaked up the sun, went for a swim, drank pina coladas and read trashy magazines together. It was girl heaven. By early afternoon the sun was scorching and Sienna decided that we needed to go shopping for our show that night. We hopped on the hotel shuttle bus and headed to the downtown shopping district that rivaled most big cities.

As was our tradition since sixth grade and we were allowed to go to the mall ourselves, we spent the first hour of our shopping excursion picking out outfits for the other to try on. I always found frumpy things for her to try on and she always made me try on the sluttiest dresses she could find. We wandered in and out of stores, our arms linked, and smiling, as we got lost in our own little world.

We eventually settled on coordinating outfits. We didn't match our outfits when we performed together, but we always coordinated something between what we wore. Sometimes it was a similar color, or a similar style. This time we found a coordinating flower and skirt length. I picked out a simple white strapless dress that hugged my curves. It was short, but not too short where I would be giving the front row a private show if the stage were more than a foot off the ground. Sienna picked out a black tank dress, with a dozen chains around the waist that hung as a belt around her hips. We bought two large hot pink flowers to put into our hair and tie our outfits together. The flowers gave us an island look.

We worked up a set list with the band that was half their regular songs and half our picks. The crowd was light at first, but the party started early for a vacation schedule. By ten thirty the crowd was big and we were getting lost in our performance. We took a break and had some water and then our first song back was one of our own originals. It was a ballad where I sang the lead and Sienna joined in on the chorus. We wrote the song in our senior year in high school, when things seemed much simpler. *Missing Half* was about a couple that meets and falls in love, and then realizes that they were each other's missing halves. I closed my eyes as I sang it and let the emotion of the words wash over me.

When the last note played, I felt drained and opened my eyes to a huge applause from the crowd. I smiled and looked around, spotting Jack leaning against the corner of a doorway staring at me. My heart skipped a beat when our eyes locked. Everyone else seemed to be applauding or smiling, but he was just standing there watching me with a serious look on his face and a drink in his hand. I directed a small smile at him and tilted my head in question toward him. He held up his drink in cheers and I watched as he drank the full glass empty.

Sienna knocked me out of my monetary haze. "Hey, that was incredible, Syd. We should do a cover song now to bring the crowd into the show. Something they know so they can join in."

I nodded and we picked an upbeat song that was popular with the drunken singalong crowds. Sienna and I took turns singing to each other and harmonized at the chorus to the song. When it was Sienna's turn to sign I scanned the crowd, looking for Jack, but he was gone. I tried not to let it upset me that he had disappeared as fast as he came, but I couldn't help but look for him the rest of the night.

We sang our last song some time after midnight and the house band continued to play. Sienna was on a high from the show and, although I'd had a great time, I was still a little disappointed that Jack hadn't stayed. Sienna ordered our usual post-show shots and a crowd gathered around us to tell us how much they'd enjoyed the show. A couple recognized Sienna from her days with the band and they bought our second round. Two handsome men complimented me on the show and asked if they could buy us our next round. Sienna accepted for both of us and we sat around talking for a while. My heart wasn't in it, but they were nice and I didn't want to be rude.

The taller of the two men asked me to dance when a slow song came on, and I politely declined. He grabbed my hand and tugged playfully at me to follow, but I was reluctant and really didn't want to go.

"Get your fucking hands off of her." Jack's voice from behind me sent a shiver up my spine.

"Mind your own business, asshole. We're just being friendly." The poor guy must have thought a random man was coming to my rescue, having misread his trying to lead me out onto the dance floor.

Jack turned me on my stool to face him, his green eyes blazing. "You want this guy touching you, babe?" His face was serious and I could see the rage barely beneath the surface.

"No, but—"

His eyes didn't leave mine but his voice was clearly directed at the guy. "Get. The. Fuck. Away. From. Her." Through the corner of my eyes I saw the guy take a few steps back, but I didn't dare look away from Jack.

"You coming with me, or do I have to carry you out of here?"

I searched his face, and I knew he was serious, yet my legs weren't moving.

He leaned in close to me. "Five, four, three...."

I jumped up and he wrapped his arm tight around my waist, pulling my body flush against his. He leaned down and kissed me. A hard, passionate and demanding kiss. He released my mouth and his arm was still wrapped tight around my waist. His other arm reached down behind my knees, lifting me up into his arms.

"What are you doing? I got up to come with you?"

"You took too long." Jack started toward the door and I heard Sienna laugh and yell, "Bye guys!"

I wrapped my arms around his neck and he carried me all the way to his room. He managed to unlock the door and open it without ever putting me down. "Did you have a good time today on your trip?" I was suddenly nervous and felt the need to talk.

"Yes." He opened the door to the bedroom and walked toward the big bed.

"How was the fishing?" I had no idea why I was desperate to suddenly make small talk.

"Good." He gently placed me down on the bed and began unbuttoning his shirt, watching me intently as I watched him.

"What did you catch?" The corners of his mouth turned up and he looked amused.

"Wahoo." He threw the shirt on the floor and reached for his belt, undoing it at a slow and steady pace.

"Did you go out on a big boat?" I must have sounded like a kid trying to stall for time to figure out what she was going to do.

"Yes." Almost a full smile.

"What time did you get back?" Not only was I asking ridiculous questions, but I was also speaking way to fast.

"Ten." He unzipped his pants and stepped out of them.

"Who caught the most fish?"

"Me." His thumbs hooked into his sexy boxer briefs and he pulled them down, revealing his fully aroused manhood. Fully naked, he took two steps toward me.

"Are you going to answer all my questions with one word?"

"Yes."

"Why?"

"Because I don't want to talk."

"Oh."

He climbed on the bed and began to pull my dress down. I wiggled to help him free it from around my hips.

"Why don't you want to talk?"

"Because I owe you slow and sweet and I really want to give it to you."

"Oh." I had no idea why I was so nervous when I had already been intimate with him, but the way he looked at me was scaring me. I wasn't afraid of him, I was afraid of what he could make me feel.

He gently covered my body with his and his mouth captured mine in a slow, sensual kiss. His tongue licked along my lips, tasting and nibbling as he slowly paid attention to every inch of my mouth. I felt his thick erection pressed up against me, throbbing on my dampened skin.

He pulled back his face to look at me, and I struggled to keep my emotions from showing. He leaned his forehead into mine and his eyes held me. His hand slowly traveled down the side of my body, caressing every curve. "I missed you today." His voice was quiet and sincere.

"Me too." I whispered softly as he looked down at me, his eyes not allowing my waiver.

His hand found my breast and he circled my nipple gently with his forefinger. My nipple puckered in anticipation of his touch. His eyes never left mine as he watched my reaction. My eyes closed on impulse as his firmly pinched my hard nipple between his forefinger and thumb. "Look at me," he commanded.

I opened my eyes and looked into his as he alternated between gently rolling and pinching my taut nipple. It felt so good, I wanted to shut my eyes and give in to the pleasure, but his eyes held mine in place. He slowly reached his head down and licked a slow, leisurely circle around the edge of my nipple, his eyes still not releasing mine. He sucked in my nipple firmly and bit down, igniting every nerve in my body. My back arched to his touch and he shifted to my other breast, repeating his slow circling and firm suck with a strong bite.

"Oh God," I moaned, and my hips pushed to find him.

He released my taut nipple and his head came back to hovering over mine. He kissed me again, sucking my tongue and taking control of the kiss. I really thought I could come from just the way he kissed me. Everything about him fueled my need, from the way he took control when he kissed me to the way he demanded I look into his eyes while he pleasured me. The thought that he was turned on by watching my reaction to him made me wild.

I wrapped my arms around his wide shoulders and dug my nails into his back. I needed more. He nibbled his way from my mouth to my shoulder, licking back up to my ear. "You are so beautiful, Syd. I want to watch you come." I wrapped my legs around his back, desperate for friction. His words brought me so close and I needed him inside me.

"Please," was the only word that I could get out. At that moment, I would have begged for him if I had to.

He took a long breath in and exhaled deeply. "Not yet." His hand slid down my torso. My body was damp with desire. "I don't want to hurt you, you're so tight." He slid one finger into me and I writhed beneath him. Two pumps of his hand and he easily slid a second finger into my slickness.

I let out a small moan as his fingers stretched me open and my head relaxed back. As he pushed into me with two fingers, his thumb found my swollen clit. My hips pushed up, begging for more. "That's it, babe, make yourself feel good." I lifted my hips and pushed against his fingers, stroking and pushing them in and out of my wet body. His thumb increased the pressure on my clit as his fingers rubbed in and out, finding a sensitive spot inside of me. My body arched to his touch and he withdrew his fingers slowly from me and brought them to my mouth. I licked the juice from his fingers and he let out a feral growl.

He positioned himself on top of me and I lifted my hips, desperate to have him inside of me. "Slow and sweet, babe, slow and sweet," he said with a raspy voice as he slowly pushed into me. His green eyes were dark gray and dilated and I knew he was having as difficult a time going slow as I was, but he wouldn't allow himself to lose control.

I gasped as he pushed deep inside of me. He was so thick and long. His eyes were full of lust and emotion, but he refused to allow them to close. The connection between us was intense and we were lost as we watched each other as he slowly pushed in and out of me, filling me to the hilt and drawing almost all the way out. His rhythm was slow and restrained and I watched his face struggle to keep the control with each deep thrust.

A deep moan escaped from my throat as my pleasure ratcheted up to new heights. His face tensed with my sound and I knew he couldn't hold his control much longer, but it felt so good and I didn't want it to end. I tilted my hips up as he thrust down and circled into me, penetrating deeper than he had ever been. He buried his face into my neck and kissed his way from my shoulder blade to my ear as he swiveled his hips, grinding his big rock hard cock into me. "Come for me, baby, I want to watch you."

His words pushed me over the edge and my body exploded in pleasure. I climaxed in a relentless spiraling orgasm that had me calling his name over and over as it tore through me. My eyes unconsciously closed as I succumbed to the waves rippling though me. "Eyes." I opened my eyes to his demand. Jack watched as it took over my body and melted me to the core. He quickened his thrusts and whispered, "Fucking beautiful," as I felt his body tense and pin me in place when he came long and hard, filling me deeply.

As we both came down, his thrusts slowed to a leisurely pace and he kissed me sweetly. "I'm sorry about last night," he said softly, as he pushed an escaped piece of my hair back from my face.

"You didn't do anything to be sorry about." It was true; he hadn't really done anything wrong, yet I understood why he was apologizing.

He looked into my eyes, searching for something, then kissed me chastely. "You're beautiful and sweet, but shit at lying, Syd."

I laughed because I knew he was right. Sienna had always told me the same thing. Jack rolled and took me with him, capturing me on top of him, my head fitting perfectly into the hollow of his shoulder. I played with the sprinkle of hair on his chest and thought about asking him more about last night and what had upset him so much, but thought better about ruining another night. Realization suddenly dawned on me that we only had two more days before I left and I had no idea when he was leaving.

"When are you scheduled to leave?" I asked bravely.

"Tomorrow at 7am." My heart stopped and I raised my head to look up at him. He looked at me with wry curved lips. "But I delayed my return flight." I released a breath that I hadn't realized that I was holding and he hugged me tightly to his chest.

"When did you postpone it to?" I whispered, afraid his answer would only leave us an extra few hours.

"That depends." His arms hugged me tighter and he kissed the top of my head. "On how many more days you are here for."

I lifted my head and propped myself up on my elbow, smiling. "You are staying until I leave?"

"Yes."

I threw myself at him, planting baby kisses all over his face. He laughed and the warm deep sound washed away my reluctance to show him how relieved I was that he was staying.

"So how many more days am I staying?" he asked, and I could hear his smile in his voice.

"Two."

"Two it is then."

The next morning I woke and found Jack already awake, watching me. He smiled at me.

"How long have you been awake?"

He lifted my hand to his mouth and kissed the palm of my hand. "Not long."

"Shower?" he asked as I stretched to unwind my body from around his.

"Caffeine," I responded on a whine.

"Addict?" He caught my earlobe between my teeth.

"Yes," I responded breathlessly from his one touch. "You?"

"Nope. No coffee, tea or soda," he stated, matter of fact. My head snapped back to him as if he had just admitted that he was a vampire and drank the blood of his victims. Who doesn't drink caffeine of some type in the morning?

"How do you wake up in the morning then?" I was almost in a cold sweat at the thought of having to start a day without at least two cups of coffee.

"I go to the gym." Ugh, one of those.

"In the morning?" I asked in an incredulous tone.

"Yes, as soon as I wake up. I either go to the gym or for a run before I start my day. I take it that isn't something that you approve of?" He was amused at my response.

"Nothing comes before caffeine in my world." I overly emphasized the word *nothing*, to add drama.

He grabbed my ass and pulled me to him, pressing his erection into me. "Nothing, huh?" A devilish smile, he smacked my ass hard. "Go get in the shower. I'll order you some coffee and breakfast. Then I'll show you what comes before caffeine when you're with me."

I rubbed my bare ass and rose in protest, making a point of prancing my naked body slowly to the bathroom. Then I turned and stuck out my tongue at him. I heard the smile in his voice as he ordered room service.

Chapter 8

After a long, thoroughly satisfying shower and some much needed caffeine and breakfast, we headed out for the day. Jack wouldn't tell me where we were headed, only that he was going to show me a few of his favorite places in Hawaii. I honestly didn't care where we were going. Jack had my fingers laced through his as he drove, the wind was in my hair, and I had spent the last twenty-four hours having the best sex of my life. I was a happy girl.

I looked over at Jack driving and he smiled at me, all perfect and beautiful and emanating raw manhood. I smiled back at him and he squeezed my hand. My thoughts ran away from me and I found myself thinking about how good he must look in a business suit with his hair slicked back. He really could model if he wanted to. I could see him with one hand in the pocket of his Christian Dior tuxedo, helping a woman with long legs out of a car in a magazine advertisement.

We pulled onto a gravel road and down a dirt path that led to very tall metal gates. A guard approached and began to ask for some id, until he recognized Jack. "Shit, Cole, I didn't know you were coming. How you been, son?"

"Good, Stephan. How is the family?" The two shook hands like old friends, although Stephan was old enough to be Jack's father. "Syd, this is Stephan. He's been with us longer than I've been around." Jack laughed and I smiled and said hello to the man.

"They're doing great. Does Caleb know you're coming, or do you want me to call ahead and tell him to get things ready for you?"

"He knows I'm coming, but thanks, Stephan. I'll see you in a few hours."

"Be careful up there, Cole."

The gates opened and Jack started down the dirt road. I could see a large building in the distance. "The way he called you Cole, it sounded like your first name. I thought Cole was your last name?"

Jack smiled. "Question number ten, babe. It's my middle name. I'm a junior and some of my father's longtime business associates started calling me Cole to avoid confusion when I was a kid. It stuck, so to the old timers I'm Cole."

"Is your father here?" After what he'd told me about his father, I didn't think we would be spending the afternoon visiting him.

Jack laughed. "No, he's not here. If he were, I wouldn't be on the island. I told you my family owns a lot of different businesses. This is one of them. I come here when I visit, and borrow some of their inventory."

I was confused at what inventory he was planning on borrowing, but quickly became distracted by the low flying helicopter almost directly above our head. The sudden loud noise scared me and I jumped in my seat.

Jack looked amused. "It's a helicopter launch area babe, I didn't mean for it to scare you."

We pulled up to a building and Jack got out and jogged around to open my door. There was something incredibly sexy about a man so demanding in the bedroom but such a gentlemen outside of it. He grabbed my hand as a man was walking over to greet us.

Jack shook hands with the man and I smiled. I couldn't hear what they were saying because of the sound coming from the helicopter that was just landing. I watched in awe as the big machine gently settled on the ground. Jack leaned in close to me and yelled, "Are you ready?" over the sound of the nearby helicopter. I shook my head, unsure if I was ready for what was really to come next. Jack grabbed my hand and led me to the helicopter, helping me in the passenger side and handing me a set of earphones, motioning for me to put them on.

Then he disappeared and I was shocked when he got in behind the pilot's seat. He put on his headphones and I watched his mouth move and heard his voice in my headphones. "You doing okay babe?"

I nodded, utterly confused. "Are you going to drive this thing?"

Jack laughed. "Yes, I'm a licensed pilot. I've been flying these since I was sixteen. You are safe with me."

He reached over and grabbed my hand, squeezing reassurance into my body.

I gave him a halfhearted attempt at a smile and he reached up and grabbed my face. "Stop worrying, I won't let anything happen to you, beautiful." Then he gave me a long slow kiss. I wasn't sure if he did it to help me relax or not, but it seemed to have worked. Jack buckled us both in and gave me one last nod before we started to go up.

It was an odd feeling to go straight up in the air. Obviously, I had flown before, but never in a helicopter. Planes go up on an angle, which is a very different feeling. We lifted off the ground and I had the strange sensation that someone was dangling us from a rope above. I was excited and terrified at the same time. My nerves didn't let me speak until our altitude leveled out and we were starting to travel forward at a steady pace.

"You okay, babe?" Jack's voice was full of concern as he looked over at me.

One of the reasons I wasn't a good liar was because my emotions showed on my face. I smiled. "I'm getting there. At least I don't feel like I am going to pass out anymore."

He reached across and grabbed my hand and squeezed it. "Try to relax and look around. This is the best way to see the island."

Tentatively, I turned my head and peeked out the window. The view was breathtaking. Turquoise water, bejeweled with vivid coral reefs contrasted against billowing white sand beaches. With how clear the water was, it looked like I could see the ocean floor. Jack pulled my hand to his mouth and kissed the top of my hand. I smiled and felt myself starting to relax a little. He pointed to the right, out my window, at a patch of green in the distance. "We're heading that way, over the rainforest." I nodded my head and smiled, a sincere smile this time.

The green forest in the distance quickly came into view and Jack circled the breathtaking coastline. As we rounded the massive forest of trees, a clearing came into vision of the most amazing tall waterfalls I had ever seen. I gasped in excitement, the picturesque scenery helping me to be rid of the last of my nerves. "That's Sacred Falls. It was the first place I flew on my own when I got my license." We flew a little further and Jack warned me that he was going to bring the helicopter down a little to show me something.

We flew lower for a few minutes and then Jack took my hand and squeezed it. "Here we go, babe." Then he raised us up dramatically along the side of huge cliffs so that it felt like we were scaling them. I couldn't help but scream in delight. It was terrifying but exciting; my adrenalin was pumping.

A little while later Jack landed us on a large open green field with no one in sight. He powered the helicopter down and came around to help me down. I jumped up and hugged him as soon as my feet reached the ground. "That was so incredible!"

Jack smiled, a sexy half smile that reached his enticing eyes, and looked pleased. He wrapped his arm around my shoulders and we walked for a while. We reached a secluded beach and took off our shoes to let the warm, crystal clear water wash over our feet as we walked. "So, you're out of questions, and I still have half of mine left."

I kicked a little water at his leg. "I guess you do."

He shook his head, but smiled. The man was utterly delicious. "Do you like pornography?"

He asked the question in the same tone as if he had just asked me to pass the salt. I tried not to blush, but I felt my face heat. I was glad we were walking so I wouldn't be subjected to his intense scrutiny as I squirmed and heated at his question. "Question number six. I guess that depends on what you are talking about. The magazines that are wrapped in plastic in the newsstands, videos of explicit sex acts, or a couple going at it on the street right in front of me?"

Jack raised an eyebrow, surprised at my response. "All of them."

His question was odd, but then, everything about the man was unpredictable. In the short time that I had known him I had learned that as soon as I thought I understood him, I was quickly proven wrong.

"Well, I don't mind the magazines, although I also don't see their allure. Let me correct my answer, I don't mind the magazine, as long as it isn't left in a bathroom. One of Michael's friends always had those types of magazines in the bathroom and it freaked me out when I went in there, wondering what he touched when he was done with the magazine."

I looked to Jack to gauge his response to my answer and he looked amused, so I continued. "As to movies, I've watched a few and I don't think they're my thing either. But perhaps I didn't watch the right ones. I guess I always felt insecure watching them, since I didn't have much experience. I also didn't get how the women could be okay with making a sex video for money. " I took a breath and tried to remember what the last part of his question was.

"And finally, as to watching sex in the street, I've never had the pleasure, so I can't tell you how I felt about it." When my answer was out, I realized it really wasn't a difficult thing to answer; it was just new to me to discuss the subject openly with anyone. Michael and I never spoke about sex, which might have been why it was so dull compared to with Jack.

"So what made you ask the question?"

Jack stopped and pulled me to his chest, wrapping his arms around my waist. He gave me a chaste kiss on the mouth and looked down at me "I'm the one asking the questions; you're all out, stranger. Come on, let's head back. I want to get us back in the air as the sun goes down."

"You know, Jack, Cole ... whatever your last name is, some women might think you were a romantic with sunset helicopter rides and long walks on the beach." I teased.

"If sharing what I enjoy with you is romantic, then I guess maybe I am. But it would only be you that would think it, because I've never shared anything more than my bed with other women."

My heart swelled a little bit. It was a good thing that we only had another day and a half, or I might have fallen head over heels for the dominating, controlling, sexy as all hell, romantic man.

Chapter 9

The next day and a half flew by as Jack and I spent almost every minute together. Most of his friends had flown back, but Tyler had extended his stay as well and the four of us enjoyed a night of dinner and slow dancing before Jack announced that we were calling it a night. We were all heading to the airport the next morning together, Sienna and I flying back to New York, with a change in Chicago, and Jack and Tyler flying to Los Angeles for a business meeting that Jack had postponed to extend his stay in Hawaii.

We were both quieter than usual, and the thought of never seeing Jack again after tomorrow made me physically sick. But I'd known from the beginning that it was only a fling and I'd gone into it with my eyes open. I'd just never expected to care for the man beneath the beautiful exterior. Our connection was more than just physical, although we couldn't keep our hands off each other. Jack had been honest about who he was from the start, and I wasn't going to ruin what we had by begging for more. But deep down inside I secretly hoped that maybe he would ask me for more, and I hated that I was setting myself up for a disastrous disappointment.

I had decided while I was getting ready that I was going to go down on Jack that night. He had taken care of me in so many ways and never asked for me to reciprocate. To most, sexual intercourse was the most intimate part of a sexual relationship, but to me oral sex was. It was something that Michael had always told me I was good at, and I had planned to show Jack how much I enjoyed my time with him in a way that I knew he would enjoy.

The two glasses of wine I had with dinner had left me feeling confident, and as soon as we were inside his room I was anxious to please him. I took his face in my hand and kissed him fiercely, as I lowered his zipper with my other hand. I reached in to his boxer briefs and ran my hand the length of his long hard shaft. He groaned, which only further ignited my frenzy to take him in my mouth. I broke the kiss and looked into his eyes. "I want to taste you."

He exhaled loudly as I dropped to my knees in front of him. I pulled his pants down the rest of the way, catching his wide head with my tongue as he moved to step out of his pants. I slowly licked the warm pre-cum glistening on the tip and looked up at him through hooded eyes. He was watching me intently, as I knew he would. I fluttered my tongue around his swollen head and licked firmly down the underside. My lips glided over his thick crown and I surprised him by taking him down in one long suck.

"Fuck," he mumbled, clearly struggling to keep his control. His arousal turned me on and fueled my performance. I wouldn't be happy until he was shattered.

I bobbed my head as I took him down, his long hard cock hitting the back of my throat. I reached for his balls and cupped him, squeezing firmly as I sucked furiously. I felt his heavy veins swell and course the length of him, as he grew thicker with each swallow.

"Jesus Christ, Syd." He grabbed my head and threaded his fingers through my hair harshly. The thought of the powerful man struggling to keep his control had me on the brink of my own orgasm. On a desperate thrust down, I swallowed, taking him even deeper into the back of my throat. That was his undoing. His hands wrapped tightly in my hair and he harshly pulled my head still as his own thrusts took over for my bobbing head. He was fucking my mouth out of a carnal need to get to his own release and it made me wild.

I had brought him to a place where he lost control and I felt powerful and satisfied. "I'm going to come, babe." His voice was gruff and raspy and sexy as hell. I grabbed his ass to let him know it was okay and he let out a ferocious growl as he spurted his hot cum into the back of my throat. He came so hard and so much that I struggled to breathe as he filled my throat with his warm thick semen. Jack didn't notice as he continued his harsh thrusts until he had emptied himself inside of me and I'd swallowed every last drop of him.

I released his deep penetration of my throat and shifted up as I licked his shaft up and down, greedily drinking in every last drop of him. Jack loosened his grip on my head and slowly unwound his fingers from my hair. He lifted me up and kissed the top of my forehead tenderly. "Smart decision to keep that to yourself until our last night, or I would never have let you leave the room."

His reaction gave me deep satisfaction. If he wasn't going to break down and profess his unbridled love for me, I at least wanted to give him something he could remember me by. "I'm glad you enjoyed it." I snuggled into his firm chest.

His hand reached down and stroked my cheek. "I enjoyed everything about this week, babe."

My heart clenched and it took everything I had not to cry at the thought of the week being over. I'd lived a fantasy for a week and I was afraid reality was never going to be able to measure up. "Me too." My voice was little more than a whisper.

We stayed awake until the sun came up, neither of us wanting to waste any of the precious time we had left. Jack made love to me while staring into my eyes with a tender possessiveness that I felt deep down in my soul. I didn't remember falling asleep, I only remembered feeling happier than I had ever been.

Chapter 10

Sienna and I finished packing in silence and she knew that I was struggling not to get upset. She had warned me to remember that it was a fling, to not become too attached, but of course I hadn't listened. Even though it had started out as purely sexual gratification, it had turned into something more, for me at least. Sienna could have said 'I told you so' when she saw my face as we pulled the last of our luggage from our room. But instead she reached out and gave me a hug. "This isn't the end of something, Syd, it's the beginning of your new life, the one you are going to lead. I know you really liked him, but there will be lots of others. You needed this to move on. So don't look back and use it to keep moving forward." She pulled back and studied my face. I had tears welled up in my eyes and fought to hold them back. "Suck those tears back, girl, crying is for wussies."

We both laughed as we followed after the bellman bringing the luggage down to meet Jack. Jack and Tyler were waiting and loaded our luggage into the car. I tried my best to act cool and nonchalant, but I knew it was written all over my face. As soon as we got on the road, Sienna reached up and took control of the radio, finding us something we enjoyed singing. I knew what she was doing, and I loved her for it. I closed my eyes and sang my heart out with Sienna as we made our way to the airport. If anything could help me change my mood, it was singing.

The drive to the airport took longer than we anticipated, and we had to rush to make it to our gate on time. Jack's flight was after ours, so he walked us to the gate and held my carry-on. The plane was already boarding when we made our way down, and I felt nauseous at having to say goodbye to him. We kissed goodbye and Jack held me tight. I cursed myself silently for not being able to fight back the tears about to escape when Jack looked at me. He searched my face and took a deep breath in.

"I still have some questions left." I couldn't respond. My stomach was in my throat and I was afraid that if I dared to speak, the tears I was somehow holding back would spill out uncontrollably.

I looked up at him in response and said nothing.

"Do you want us to be over?"

"No." I shook my head as I spoke. A tear escaped and traveled slowly down my face. Jack wiped my tear away gently with his fingers, caressing my cheek.

The flight attendant announced final boarding and Sienna yelled at me to move my ass. Jack kissed

me again once more and when I turned back as I went
down the jetway, he was still watching me.

Chapter 11

"Can I get you something to drink?"

Startled out of my daydream by the perky flight attendant, it took me a minute to snap out of my thoughts. I was in such a fog that I couldn't be sure if I had just woken, and the last week had been just a dream, or if it was really an unforgettable memory.

"I'll have a vodka cranberry and she'll have a merlot. You'll have to excuse her, she's spent the last week fucking her brains out with a gorgeous stranger and can't seem to snap out of it." Sienna smiled to the appalled flight attendant, a pleasant-looking mid-forties woman who was wearing way too many pins on her bulging uniform. From the look on her face, I was sure the flight attendant wasn't used to a raunchy-mouth like Sienna in first class. I looked around and saw most of the other passengers looked well bred and refined, more like they were dressed for an uppity tennis match than a twelve hour flight from Honolulu to New York.

The flight attendant brought us our drinks and scurried away with a hesitant smile. It was obvious she was trying to avoid hearing any more about our vacation, which Sienna would have surely divulged if given the opportunity. Sienna enjoyed shocking uptight people with her crass mouth. Watching them squirm was a sport for her.

Sienna raised her glass to me in a toast. "To the best damn honeymoon I've ever been on." I laughed and shook my head as we clinked glasses and both tipped our heads back to drink.

"Seriously, Syd, are you okay? I know the week meant more to you than just a fling."

I took a deep breath and gathered my thoughts. "Maybe I just got caught up in the fantasy of it all. A beautiful island, a gorgeous man, it was easy to think it was all real." I downed the rest of my drink. "I mean, I don't even know his last name."

Sienna took my hand and held it in hers. "It's probably for the best, Syd. You need to figure out what you want to do before getting too involved with another guy anyway." I knew she was right, but it didn't make it hurt any less.

The uptight flight attendant came by to ask if we wanted another drink and her eyes went straight to our joined hands. Sienna, being Sienna, raised our joined hands to her mouth and kissed the back of my hand while looking at the flight attendant. "What, you never saw a couple in love? I told you we were on our way back from our honeymoon?" As was common when Sienna got the urge, the woman walked away speechless.

Chapter 12

A week after our return home from Hawaii I was no more settled than I was the morning I walked away from Jack in the airport. I just couldn't get him out of my head. I replayed the week over and over in my mind and couldn't help but think that Jack was feeling the same thing for me as I was for him. What if he was my one true love and I let him slip away because of some ridiculous notion that I couldn't find the love of my life just because it had started out as a rebound fling? I alternated hourly how I felt. There were mornings that I held the phone in my hand, seriously considering calling the hotel in Hawaii and begging them to get in touch with Jack and give him my number. But then there were afternoons where I came to the realization that I had spent the week with a playboy who probably had weeks like we'd shared on a regular basis.

My honeymoon was over and I went back to work, but I knew that I wasn't singing with the gusto that I should have been. I was going through the motions and giving mediocre performances that would more than likely have me destined for eternal damnation as a lounge singer. I needed to refocus myself and find a way to use my singing as an outlet for my heartbreak.

As usual, I arrived at the hotel two hours before the club opened to set up and practice. I was in the middle of my second practice song when the hotel general manager stopped in and asked me to come to his office for a quick meeting. My gut wrenched and I was sure that I was going to be fired for my lackluster performances.

Lyle Coughlin, the hotel manager, was a thirty-something yuppie wannabe who might have been cute if he wasn't so damn full of himself. He wore expensive suits and shiny shoes and treated most of the employees like they were his servants. I had heard from one of the barmaids that he only had the job because he was related to the Heston family through marriage. I knocked at his door and he yelled for me to enter. "Come in, Sydney, have a seat." He motioned to one of the leather chairs on the opposite side of his desk.

He came around the desk and lifted one leg to sit on the edge of the corner of the desk close to me, folding his hands into his lap. I was sure that before I arrived at his office, Lyle had thoroughly deliberated on the exact position that he should sit while we spoke in order for him to look as authoritative as possible during our talk. It was just the kind of pompous ass he was. "So, Sydney, how do you like it here at the Heston?"

Why couldn't the asshole just fire me and get it over with instead of dragging it out? I plastered on my best fake smile and said, "Oh, I love it here. The clientele is very posh and I enjoy performing in the Overture Club." I didn't really think the clientele was posh; in fact, I hated the freaking word posh. But I knew it would be what the arrogant asshole wanted to hear, so I had to try to salvage my job.

"Good, good. I'm glad to hear it. Well, you must be doing something right. Mr. Heston has informed me that he will be coming to your show tonight. He mentioned that he has heard many good things about you and wanted to see for himself." Lyle stood, leaning against the desk with his ankles crossed and arms folded across his chest, posturing himself as a parent would when they were giving a child a reward for good behavior. I wouldn't have been surprised if the asshole patted me on the head. "So, Sydney, I don't have to tell you how important tonight's show is. Mr. Heston is a busy man and this hotel is a reflection on him, so everything needs to be perfect tonight."

Ummm, not too much pressure.

Lyle walked back around the desk and motioned his arm that he was finished. I was a minion who was being dismissed. "I'll be at your performance tonight also. Break a leg, Sydney."

Great, I thought, *now I have to change up my performance for the old rich guy. What does one sing to a wealthy old man?* I suddenly had pictures of myself dressing up in the infamous white Marilyn Monroe dress and softly singing *Happy Birthday, Mr. President* to a seventy-five year old crotchety hotel mogul sitting with a twenty year old ditzy buxom blonde clinging to his arm.

As if she was reading my mind, my phone buzzed with a text from Sienna. *Hey rock chick, plans for tonight? Let's go to that Piano Bar on 55th when you get off for a few? I'm having Syd withdrawals. U up for it? XO Si*

Her texts always brightened my day. When I was with Michael he would get annoyed at how often we would text back in forth, but it never stopped us. *Sounds good. BTW what do I perform for an old rich hotel mogul that is coming to see my show tonight?*

Two seconds later. *Oral sex, man's favorite performance at any age.*

I'd walked right into that one. *While that's tempting, I was thinking more along the lines of a singing performance than a humming one. LOL.*

He's old huh? Since you've been gone ... Aretha baby. Your voice kicks that song's ass! XOXO Meet you at midnight?

Perfect, thanks! TTYL Xo Syd

I went about my routine and did a few practice songs when the band arrived. They were impressed with my rendition of *Since You've Been Gone*, so I was glad that Sienna has suggested it. I wasn't really nervous about singing in front of Mr. Heston, I had sung in front of large crowds and I didn't often get stage fright. But the reality was that I was broke, and his opinion mattered because I needed my job. I had been an idiot about my finances when I left Michael. I'd left him everything, even our joint savings account. At the time, it was a pride thing; I didn't want to admit that I needed anything from him or us, so I left with just my clothes. Now I was starting to think that taking half the savings and some of the furniture would have been the smarter thing to do. But it was too late now, and I was determined to make it on my own one way or another.

The crowd started to roll in slowly during my first set. I wasn't sure what Mr. Heston looked like, but I didn't see anyone that could be him. I knew Lyle would be making a big fuss over him and the staff was all on high alert to attend to his every need.

Two songs into my second set, I spotted Lyle sitting at a table set in the front, a little bit off to the side. He must have come in on my break, because I hadn't noticed him earlier. He was sitting with a man older than him, but not quite the definition of a crotchety old hotel mogul that I had in my head. The man was probably in his fifties, with salt and pepper hair and masculine strong features. He was distinguished and handsome and his face was vaguely familiar, although I couldn't place where I knew him. I thought perhaps that the two men were still waiting for Mr. Heston and the other gentleman was also an employee of Heston Hotels.

A few songs later I was near the end of my set and there was still no sign of Mr. Heston. I belted out the Aretha song that I had added for the old man and said goodnight to the crowd. On the weekends the band had to stay to play for another hour, but after my singing ended they took the volume down and stuck to background music.

Lyle called from his table as I was leaving the stage. The man truly had no manners. How difficult would it have been to walk a few steps over and ask me over to his table? Pushing my thoughts of the pompous ass aside, I put on my best fake smile and walked to his table. The gentleman that he was seated with stood as I approached, forcing Lyle to follow suit, which I secretly enjoyed. Lyle would never have thought to stand when a woman approached on his own.

"Sydney, this is Mr. Heston." I looked to the gentleman and tried to hide my surprise. Damn, the old guy was even better up close. He had light green eyes that stood out against his tan skin, which I hadn't noticed earlier because of the light glare on stage.

"Hello, nice to meet you, Mr. Heston." We shook hands and Lyle invited me to sit with them.

"What can I get you to drink, Sydney?" Mr. Heston ignored Lyle's empty glass in front of him when the waitress approached.

"Just a water, please. My throat needs to cool down after I perform and adding alcohol has the opposite effect." I felt the need to give an explanation so I wouldn't insult the man who stood between me and paying my rent next month.

He nodded and gave his order for scotch to the waitress. Lyle began talking about the upcoming annual Heston shareholder meeting and how honored I should be that Mr. Heston had taken time out of his busy schedule to come see me sing. I nodded and smiled and did my best to look interested as he spoke. But I found the way that Mr. Heston was looking at me to be distracting. It wasn't lewd or improper; rather I got the feeling he was looking for something in me, watching me, observing.

At some point, Mr. Heston got bored of Lyle talking too and I was grateful when he interrupted him mid-sentence. "I really enjoyed your show, Sydney. How would you like to perform at our annual shareholder meeting next week? We were supposed to have some famous boy band, but I hate that crap and I find you to be captivating when you sing. I know it's short notice, but if you are free next weekend, I'll messenger over a contract tomorrow and let my assistant know about the change."

"Wow, that sounds great. I have a few things lined up for next weekend, but I'm sure I can rearrange them." Damn it, I'd have to rearrange that bubble bath I was planning on taking next weekend. No one wants an artist that isn't in demand.

He smiled at me and threw back his drink. He stood, giving me a glimpse of the rest of him, and I couldn't help but notice the whole package was pretty damn good. Tall, fit and broad shouldered, he wore low-hanging navy blue trousers and a French blue tailored dress shirt that looked as if he had recently opened the collar and removed the tie. If only I was a few years older....

"It was very nice to meet you, Sydney. He leaned in close as he shook my hand and lowered his voice. "And I'm a big Aretha fan, so let's keep that one for next week, shall we?" He winked and released my hand. I watched as he left, and the view was as good going as it was coming.

Sienna was sitting at the piano playing and singing when I walked into our agreed-upon bar. A crowd sat around her at the piano; some of them probably thought that she worked there. I had no idea what she had done with the pianist, but it was typical Sienna. "Do I need to look for the pianist tied and gagged somewhere?" I raised one eyebrow in question.

Her painted red lips and glossy white teeth smiled up at me in sharp contrast to her pale skin. "Get your skinny ass over here and join me, babe." Sienna scooted her butt over to make room for me at the piano bench. It didn't take long before we had the entire bar singing *I Will Survive* along with us. My mom had always said that Sienna and I were contagious. We were always able to get lost in the moment and have fun when we were together, and somehow, others always joined in.

Sienna stood up after we ended the song and took a dramatic bow, her unruly curls flopping all over as she flipped her head up and down. "Cover for me for a while, Lenny." She turned and spoke to the regular piano player as if she was the employee and he was helping her out. I was also pretty sure his name wasn't even Lenny.

We laughed our way up to the bar and ordered our usual tequila shots. I told her about Mr. Heston coming to see me sing and his offer for me to sing at their shareholder meeting instead of the previously booked boy band. She was excited and told me about a potential gig that she was working on for us to sing together at the wedding of one of the NY Yankees.

A tall dark haired man approached as we spoke and stood next to me. He was polite enough to wait until a break in our conversation before he interrupted. "You ladies were great. Can I buy you both a drink?" His question was directed at both of us, but he spoke to me directly.

"Thank you, but not tonight. We are having a girls night."

He pretended to clutch his heart in pain. "That's too bad. But you ladies have a good one anyway." He politely excused himself and walked away. Most men didn't take rejection well, especially in a bar after a few drinks when their friends were nearby, so I never knew what to expect.

"So, Syd, are you still lusting after Jack so much that you didn't even notice that one was cute?" Trust Sienna to always be direct.

I sighed. "I'm trying to move on, but it's not that easy. When I left Michael I felt a loss for the routine, the normalcy, but not really for him as a man. I didn't crave his touch or wake up in a cold sweat after dreaming I was still with him."

Sienna looked at me wide-eyed. "Shit, Syd, you got it bad. I thought it was just emotional because he was your first after Michael. Are you in love with him?"

I thought about our night under the stars, lying on our backs holding hands and talking. I thought about our sweaty bodies slapping against each other as we furiously tried to get closer as we came together. A dazed smile crept across my mouth as I stared at the mental images burned into my brain, but I didn't give her an answer.

Sienna took a cigarette from the pack in front of the man sitting next to her and smiled. He turned and flicked a lighter, flaming the cigarette that she'd bummed without asking.

I leaned over Sienna to the man next to her. "Can I have one of those please?" I extended my two fingers to him to place the cigarette between.

"You don't smoke," Sienna stated matter-of-factly with one eyebrow arched quizzically.

The man lit my cigarette and I took a deep inhale, letting out a long puff of smoke on a deep exhale. "Neither do you." We both smiled at each other.

Chapter 13

The Heston annual shareholder meeting was being held in the main ballroom of the five stars Heston Grand in Times Square. I had expected gaudy and extravagant, but was pleasantly surprised to find eloquent and understated. Lyle had told me that presidents usually stayed at the hotel when they were in town, as it often hosted fundraisers for wealthy donors. The contract had come earlier in the week, as Mr. Heston had promised, and I was pleasantly surprised at the generous fee that I was being paid for my services. It was more than three months pay for my regular job singing at the Heston hotel, but I wasn't going to complain even though I did think it was excessive for the three songs that I'd been hired to sing.

The event coordinator had contacted me the week before and informed me that the gala was black tie and that I was expected to wear an evening gown. I was relieved to find out that the cost of the gown was borne by Heston Hotels, because although I had some really nice dresses, I had nothing that could be classified as an evening gown.

I still had a light tan from our trip to Hawaii, so I picked a light blue sequin dress that was form fitting. The front was simple and had a V-neck that showed some cleavage, but couldn't be described as plunging. The back, however, was the showstopper. It plunged deep into my back, barely covering the top of the crack of my ass. It was beautiful and sexy, yet elegant and classy. The sales clerk had assured me that the sequins would reflect the stage lights and dazzle the audience. The color reminded me of the strapless dress that I'd worn in Hawaii and I smiled, thinking back to Jack's reaction when he'd seen me in it.

I watched from the side of the stage as the ballroom filled up with men in tuxedos and women in beautiful ball gowns. It struck me as odd that an annual shareholder meeting would be so formal, but the fancy clothing gave the ballroom a magical feeling and the celebration was, after all, for a high-end hotel group.

When the MC announced my name, I suddenly thought it might have been a mistake to pair the dress with five-inch stilettos, but I made it to the microphone unscathed. I knew the ballroom was packed, but the size of the crowd never bothered me. The lighting usually blinded the audience from me anyway. Something about being unable to see people's faces made it easy for me to get lost in a song and allow myself to feel the music through my body.

I performed two songs at the beginning of the meeting and then the final song was a repeat of the Aretha song that Mr. Heston had requested, and it closed the meeting. The crowd was gracious enough to give me a standing ovation, but I figured they were also anxious to get up from such a long conference.

Backstage, the conference producer looked way more relieved than she had a few hours earlier. She was laughing and smiling and finally had that awful headset unglued from her head. All of the stage crew and the MC gathered backstage and opened a few bottles of champagne to celebrate the success of the conference. I was mingling with some of the lighting crew, enjoying my post-show high with a glass of good champagne, when I felt a hand on my bare back.

"Sydney, you were fantastic tonight. Thank you for putting on such a great show on such short notice." Mr. Heston spoke with impeccable grammar that screamed expensive private schooling, and it made me stand a bit straighter.

"Mr. Heston, thank you very much, that is very kind of you. I had a great time and it looks as though your conference was a rousing success." The hand holding my champagne motioned to the crew, happily celebrating.

"What. The. Fuck?" The growl came from behind me and sent my body into an instant frenzy. I didn't have to turn to know it was Jack, but I was suddenly desperate to catch a glimpse of him again. I turned and saw the beautiful creature stalking towards us. At first

I didn't even notice the woman following behind him, struggling to keep up.

Mr. Heston turned with me, his hand still on my bare back. For a second I thought Jack might leap forward and attack the poor man. Jack came to a screeching halt before us and his eyes shot daggers at Mr. Heston, tracing the hand now pressing harder on my bare skin. Was he jealous? The man had made no attempt to contact me for almost three weeks and now was showing up where I was working to make a scene like a raving lunatic.

"I'll ask one more time. What the fuck are you doing?" Jack spoke directly to Mr. Heston and his tone made me nervous about what was about to happen.

I finally found my voice and it was more than a little angry. "Jack, this is Mr. Heston. He owns this hotel and hired me to sing tonight."

His eyes never left Mr. Heston's when he spoke. "He owns HALF of the voting stock of the hotel. And I don't know what kind of game you are playing, but maybe you should remember who owns 51% and who owns 49%, Dad." Jack uttered *Dad* with so much hatred and disdain, it was as if a blow had physically been thrown.

"I don't know what you are talking about, son." Mr. Heston spoke low in a cool as ice voice. He was obviously concerned with people hearing, as Jack's tirade had already caught the attention of most of the crew backstage.

Their words took a moment, but finally registered

in my stunned brain. "This is your father?" My voice trembled as I spoke.

Jack took one step forward and spoke in Mr. Heston's face. "Get your filthy fucking hands off her now."

Mr. Heston immediately removed his hand from my back, which I had forgotten was even still there. The two men stared at each other for a moment in silence, unspoken threats passing. Then Jack put out his hand to me. I looked at his face and knew I didn't have a choice, even if he was scaring me. I put my hand in his and he clamped his long fingers around my hand and turned to walk.

He said nothing as I trailed behind him, my hand cupped so tightly in his that my fingers began to get numb. When we passed the woman that had followed him backstage, he spat at her, "Go home, Jenna." I eyed her as we passed. She was wearing a red dress that was incredibly revealing and her huge obviously fake breasts looked as if they might burst out at any second. She was attractive, but in an odd, overly made-up sort of way, the kind of look that is done on purpose to stand out and scream that you aren't the girl next door.

Jack raced through the hallways with purpose, only slowing enough to let me catch up so that I wouldn't fall on my face. Men in tuxedos passed as we walked by, each trying fruitlessly to catch Jack's attention or exchange a greeting. Jack ignored them as if they didn't exist. We arrived at the elevator banks and waited in silence. As the car arrived, Jack put his hand on my bared back to direct me forward and that jolt of electricity I hadn't felt since Hawaii ran through me. He put a key into the elevator and I watched as he pressed the button for the penthouse.

The elevator doors opened directly to an apartment and Jack attempted to lead us inside, but my feet were frozen in place. I still hadn't looked at him. "Where are we?" I whispered, needing assurance about something.

"My apartment; I live here." He stood in place behind me and waited with the elevator doors open. He wasn't going to force me inside. I hesitantly stepped forward and out of the car.

I stayed just in front of the elevator doors as they closed behind me. My head was reeling and I was confused at all that had happened. Jack's father was Mr. Heston? Jack clearly hadn't known I was performing at the conference, so was it just a coincidence that his father had hired me? Somehow I didn't think so. And why was Jack so angry? I felt like a pawn in a game that I had never agreed to play.

Eventually Jack walked around me and into the open space. I looked up to see where he was going and watched him walk into a huge open modern kitchen. He leaned against the island counter, his hands behind his neck, clenched. My eyes took him in, I hated that I couldn't help but notice how beautiful he looked in his tuxedo. His wide shoulders filled the black jacket and I knew that hidden beneath was a thick strong muscular body that I wanted to touch.

After a few minutes in silence, he looked up at me. His green eyes piercing straight through to my heart. He studied my face, as I studied him. "Did you know he was my father?"

"No." My voice was merely a whisper. "Isn't your date going to look for you?"

"I only brought her to piss off my father. It's what I do." Jack's voice was filled with regret.

He took a deep breath in and studied me for another minute. I watched as the battle within his mind played out on his face. He was angry and struggling with something. He stalked to me and picked me up, lifting me at the knees into his two hands, and I let him. Neither of us said a word as he carried me and kicked open his bedroom door and laid me on the bed.

Jack's face was still angry and tense as he hovered over me. I wanted to tell him to fuck off, and ask him why he hadn't tried to contact me for three weeks. But every nerve in my body was electrified, a traitor to my brain. I wanted to ask him if he had missed me as much as I missed him, but I was afraid of the answer.

I couldn't take his intense stare anymore, I knew I was ready to break. Emotions were flooding me fast — anger, confusion, and the worst of them all, lust at the sight of the gorgeous man. I turned my head just as the first tear escaped. I suddenly wanted to run away from him and not let him see me that way. But just as I turned my head away from him, he turned his too and his mouth closed the inches between us and covered mine. It wasn't a soft building kiss, it was gas meeting fire. The outpouring of all the pent-up emotions in one hair-raising, hard, frantic kiss. Somehow we managed to pull off each other's clothes without breaking for air. The minute my hands touched his bare back all thought escaped my mind, except having him inside me.

I trailed my nails down the skin of his hot, sleek, hard back, digging in to bring pain. I don't know why, but I needed him to feel me, feel my pain and my pleasure. I had never had the urge to bring pain to another person before, but I couldn't control myself. I felt his mouth tense as I scarred his back and he bit into my lip in response. The pain sent pleasure down to my throbbing clit instantly.

He rolled us until I was on top of him, one leg straddling each side of his thick thighs. I sucked in his lip and bit down. I was so engrossed in the kiss that I didn't see his hand coming. His large right hand connected firmly with my ass, making a loud smack. The sting made my eyes water but my body reacted to the pain without warning. I was on the verge of an orgasm and I needed him inside of me so badly it hurt. I rubbed my swollen clit over his long hard cock, desperately seeking friction. I tried to reach down and grab him in my hand so that I could put him inside me, but Jack grabbed my wrists and flipped us again so that he was back on top.

With my arms pinned to my sides by his weight, his head dipped and his mouth greedily covered my nipple. His tongue lashed and swirled and he bit down hard, elongating my already swollen nub. I moaned in response and tried to grab at him, but my arms didn't move under his strength. He licked his way over to my other nipple, applying the same torture. He bit down until my breath caught, and then sucked in deep. He didn't release me until it started to burn and I was panting uncontrollably.

He buried his head into my neck and rammed himself deep into me without warming. I gasped. He was so hard and deep, but it still wasn't enough. I wanted more. I needed more. He pulled almost all the way out, leaving just the tip inside of me and then slammed into me hard again, his balls slapping into my ass. I was desperate for more of him and grinded my hips up to rock into him, but he pinned me back into place with his body. He slammed into me over and over again until our bodies were dripping in sweat and we were both panting for air.

He reached around and lifted my ass into his thrusts, adjusting the angle to go even deeper. His cock rubbed that place inside of me that cried out for him, until my body tightened and I began to climax. I shuddered at his words, "Look at me," as my body spiraled longer and harder than I ever imagined was possible. Jack watched me intently as he drained every last reflex from my body before allowing himself to empty inside of me.

I have no idea how long we laid tangled in each other's arms. I was exhausted and my body and mind were bruised and battered.

The next morning I woke with an aching feeling in the pit of my stomach. I reached to my side and touched the cold bed. Jack was gone. I laid still, listening for signs that he was still there, but my heart knew the answer before my brain caught up with it. After an hour of allowing my mind to pretend that Jack had only gone out for breakfast for us and was coming back, I dragged myself out of bed. The only thing I had to wear was my evening gown from the night before, so I found Jack's tuxedo shirt from the night before and put it on. It hung to my knees and I stupidly allowed my senses to take in Jack's smell as I closed my eyes.

I walked through the penthouse. It was all unfamiliar from the night before, except the kitchen. I knew there was no note, but I allowed myself to look for one so that I wouldn't spend the next month beating myself up that there could have been one that I missed. It was almost 11 o'clock on Sunday morning and even I couldn't convince myself that Jack had ran out for pressing business.

I snooped around for a little bit, amazed at the expanse of the place that he lived. There were three bedrooms and five bathrooms. Why would one man possibly need five bathrooms? The master bath off of his bedroom was larger than my apartment and had a view of Times Square. I remembered that Jack's friend Tyler had commented that Jack was wealthy, but I couldn't have comprehended the magnitude of that statement at the time.

I searched in his closet for something to wear, dreading the thought of doing the walk of shame through the hotel in my evening gown on a Sunday morning. I decided on his tuxedo shirt and a pair of black compression shorts to make my escape. Luckily I had packed flip flops in my purse, knowing it might take me a few blocks to find an available cab in Times Square after my performance.

I didn't have a problem hailing a cab right in front of the hotel and I even made it out without too many odd looks. Walking around Times Square in a man's tuxedo shirt and compression shorts, while holding an evening gown, didn't even raise any eyebrows compared to the really crazy looking people out there.

Chapter 14

My days off were usually Sunday and Monday, so I had two full days for my pity party. I spent the balance of Sunday going over the last twenty-four hours in my head. Monday morning I was convinced that Jack was my destiny and I needed to find him, needed to confront him and make him see the light. By Monday evening I had decided that he was a bipolar sexual deviant and if he ever tried to come near me again I would get a restraining order. Needless to say, I was confused and distraught and I was left with no choice but to fess up to Sienna and seek counseling.

All it took was one simple text. *Had a bad night Saturday night ... saw Jack, slept with him, he disappeared again.* She was at my door in less than half an hour with a bottle of tequila, two quarts of Ben and Jerry's, and her guitar.

"Spill, babe, and start from the beginning. We have all night." Sienna grabbed two shot glasses from the kitchen, which were, incidentally, also the housewarming gift that she gave me when I moved to New York last month. She plopped herself down on the couch, cracked open the tequila, poured us shots, and I started at the beginning.

As I told my tale, I added in bits and pieces about Jack's relationship with his dad that I had learned on our trip to Hawaii. By the time I was done, and we had analyzed everything that had transpired, we were both convinced that Jack's dad had known who I was somehow and was using me in some sort of demented game he was playing.

There truly was no better friend in life than Sienna. She was pissed at anyone who didn't adore me, and hated anyone who screwed with me, without question. I found it interesting that my best friend knew more about my relationship with Jack, that had transpired over an eight day period, than she did about my relationship with Michael, which had lingered over seven years. Why did I share so much about Jack with her, yet I'd never felt the need to talk about Michael, even after a fight?

I started to wonder why my eight day relationship meant so much more to me than my seven year relationship with the man that I had planned to marry. Had I ever really loved Michael, or was he just my safe place? As I rewound time in my head I realized that Michael had never taken my breath away. He'd never made my heart beat out of my chest so loud that I thought the whole world could hear it. And he'd certainly never made my body quiver uncontrollably with just a kiss. Jack did, and the realization tore my heart out.

Chapter 15

The week went by slowly and each day I walked into the Heston it got harder. The hotel reminded me of Jack and what we'd had together. What I had lost, again. Luckily, Lyle didn't find out what had happened backstage after the conference. Or at least he didn't mention it to me if he had heard. He did, however, tell me that Mr. Heston's office had called to tell him that I did a great job and that Mr. Heston was very satisfied. I really didn't care what Mr. Heston thought, but I was grateful his call seemed to make Lyle happy, which meant he left me alone all week.

Friday night the hotel club was extra busy and the band convinced me to stay an extra hour past the end of my normal shift to keep the crowd partying. I was drained from the long week without contact from Jack, but agreed to stay anyway. I was becoming good friends with the guys in the band and we seemed to have found our stride together. The drummer, Travis, and I had even had lunch together twice, and when we were working he established himself as my resident bodyguard.

Travis Toomey didn't look like a typical hotel club band drummer. He had long dark brown hair pulled back into a ponytail, a goatee, and what could only be described as dark brown almond-shaped bedroom eyes. His arms were covered in tattoos and he was physically enormous. He towered above most people with his six foot six frame and shoulders that spanned the width of two regular-sized men. When I first saw him sitting behind the drums, I remember thinking that he made the full-size drum kit look like he was playing a children's set. His handsome face was marred by a deep scar going the length from just beneath his eye to his chin. He looked like he just gotten out of jail and had ridden to the bar on his motorcycle to find a woman, club her over the head, and drag her out the back door, unconscious. He looked the epitome of the phrase *dark and dangerous.*

But the truth of the matter was that Travis rode a bicycle to work and was married to Tom, a man he had been with for more than ten years. He didn't care what people thought and I was pretty sure he liked people to think that he was a rough and tumble badass. It worked for me because I had seemingly become a magnet for drunk single men who thought I would be sufficiently impressed by their slurring pick-up lines. Travis always kept an eye out for me and would come to my rescue by putting his arm around my shoulder and calling me babe. Every man quietly disappeared with his tail between his legs within thirty seconds of Travis's appearance.

Travis also always walked me outside and waited until I was safely in a cab before leaving. Friday night there were extra crazies out in the city at one in the morning, so I was grateful that Travis was such a good friend. He kissed me gently on the cheek before I folded into the cab and he gave a sour warning to the driver to take good care of "his woman."

An hour later I was drifting off to sleep when I was startled back to consciousness by a loud banging at my door. It wasn't a normal knock. Before I even made it three steps from my bed, the person on the other side of the door was pounding my door again furiously. Thoughts ran through my head: there was a fire in my building, or a neighbor was being attacked and needed help.

I opened the door a crack and left the chain on for safety. I probably should have asked who it was first, but I was reacting to the anxious knocking at the door and wasn't thinking. My pounding heart stopped dead when I saw Jack standing there, his forehead pressed to the doorjamb, which was holding him up. I wasn't afraid of him physically, but I didn't release the chain either.

His beautiful green eyes were bloodshot when they locked on me. "Can I come in?"

I could smell the liquor on his breath as he spoke

and his words were slightly slurred. A pause and then, "Please."

I looked into his eyes and saw sadness and pain. I nodded my head and released the safety chain. He walked in slowly, never taking his eyes off of me. We stood there for a moment, facing each other, just looking and watching each other's reactions. His hand slowly reached for my hip and I took a step backwards. He flinched at my reaction and balled his hands into tight fists at his sides.

"Is that why you are here? A middle of the night booty call?" I was becoming more and more pissed off each second.

"No." His voice was defensive, but he dropped his head in shame.

"So why are you here then?"

His eyes lifted from the floor to find mine. "I don't know. I just couldn't keep away."

Jack's words touched me and I let my guard slip slightly. My words were no longer bitter, but I still needed to know more. "Why did you leave and not come back last weekend?"

He visibly flinched again at my question. I watched as he thought and his eyes filled with emotion. "Because I'm a fucking horrible man and you deserve better."

For me, alcohol was my truth serum, and I hoped it was the same for Jack. "Why are you a horrible man?"

He looked tortured and conflicted and I couldn't bear it any longer. I reached out my hand to him to provide comfort. I saw relief flood his eyes. He took my hand and held it, waiting for me to allow him something more. "I have no idea how to have a relationship." A long pause. "I hate my father for who he is, but I'm just like him."

I couldn't bear anymore. I needed to take away his pain, even after all the pain he had caused me. I closed the space between us and laid my head to his chest, wrapping my arms around his waist tightly. His arms wrapped around me, engulfing me into his pain. I listened with my ear at his chest as his racing heartbeat slowed and he clung to me tightly.

We stayed that way for a long time. My emotions were running wild, but I felt more alive than I had that whole week. I pulled back to look at his face, and I could tell he was reluctant to loosen his grip. His face was full of concern. "Would you like to stay and talk in the morning?"

Jack didn't respond with words; instead he pulled me back into his arms and wrapped me inside of his hold even tighter. I brought him to my bedroom and sat him on the edge of the bed. I reached down and removed his shoes. He watched me hesitantly, making no move to touch me. He was afraid of overstepping his place for fear I would change my mind.

"Do you want to take off your pants?"

He looked at me and shook his head no, but reached for me as he lay back on the bed and positioned me with my head on his chest, his arms wrapped around me so tightly I couldn't move if I wanted to. But I didn't want to move. I hated to admit it, but there was nowhere else I would have rather been.

The next morning Jack was still sleeping when I woke up. His sleep only slightly loosened his hold on me and I had to pry myself from his arms in order to get up. He stirred when I snuck out of bed, but eventually he settled back into sleep. Nature was calling, and I needed an extra large cup of coffee and two aspirin for my pounding headache.

I decided to make bacon and eggs, hoping that Jack would stay for breakfast this time and make good on his promise to talk in the morning. I sang softly to myself, trying not to wake him. I didn't know how to cook without singing. In fact, there were a lot of things that I found physically impossible to do without at least quietly humming a tune.

I turned the bacon and caught Jack standing in the doorway out of the corner of my eye. His frame filled the doorway and he rested his arms on the doorjambs as he watched me.

"Good morning." I spoke quietly, suddenly aware that I was still only wearing my old Yankee t-shirt that barely covered my ass. Michael was a diehard Red Sox fan and hated the shirt, which was probably why I had made it into my official pajamas most nights since moving to New York.

"Good morning." His voice was raspy and deep and sexy as hell.

I smiled at him. "Hungry?"

"Starving." His tone told me we might not be speaking about the same thing. He made no attempt to move into the kitchen, appearing content in watching me.

"You just going to stand there and watch me?" One eyebrow arched questioningly.

"I am." The corner of his mouth turned slightly up, hinting at a smile.

I shook my head and laughed, turning my attention back to the stove. He didn't move from his position until I placed our plates on the table.

We sat together at the table and ate our breakfast and it felt so normal and right. "How did you know where I lived?" So many unanswered questions rattled through my brain.

"Your personnel file."

My face clearly showed my astonishment. "If you own half of the Heston, I guess that does technically make you my employer, doesn't it?"

"It does." He made no attempt to hide his lack of feeling guilty for using his position for his personal needs. The hesitant, insecure man from the night before was gone and confident, alpha Jack was back with a vengeance.

"I take it you didn't know I was performing at the conference?"

"Definitely not."

"Why did your father hire me?"

"I have no idea. I've got a call into the resort in Honolulu to find out if he made contact with anyone there."

The Hawaii resort had never crossed my mind. But it dawned on me that we had stayed at one of the hotels he owned, explaining why everyone had known his name. I stood to clear the table and Jack grabbed my arm, gently pulling me into his lap.

"I like your t-shirt." He looked down at me on his lap. My shirt rode up over my skimpy underwear. His warm hand cautiously moved to my thigh. As always, his touch sent a jolt through my body. I needed to separate my body from his or we would never have that talk.

"Yankees fan?" I jumped out of his lap. It was obvious what I was doing and he seemed amused at the reaction that I was having.

"Now I am." His voice was low and gravely and I felt his eyes burning into my back as I stood with my back to him, rinsing the dishes. I took my time, hoping the fire inside me would quell with distance.

Jack knew what I was doing and wasn't going to allow it. I felt the heat from his body behind me and his breath on my neck. He stood with his front to my back, only inches separating us.

"Can I touch you, Syd?" I knew it must have been difficult for him to ask permission. Jack wasn't the type of man that asked. He took what he wanted.

My mind was foggy from his close proximity and my answer came out breathless. "Yes."

His hand brushed over my breast and I had to grip the edge of the counter to keep my weak knees from buckling. The man made me feel like a teenager getting touched for the first time.

Unlike last time, his touch was soft and gentle, but it turned me on no less. He kneaded my tender breasts and circled my nipples, his thumb brushing gently over my stiff peaks. Jack pushed his body firmly against my back and I felt his hardness up against my ass. A moan escaped from deep in my throat and I heard Jack growl.

His lips trailed kisses up and down the back of my neck, then he licked his way to my ear. He nibbled my lobe and his hot fast breath sent a wave of pleasure from my ear down to my already swollen clit.

One of his hands found its way to my sex and my legs widened shamelessly at his unspoken command. I was aroused and panting as one hand hovered near my clit while the other pinched at my swollen nipples.

"I love how wet you get for me" Jack whispered in my ear as he slid his hand beneath my panties and pushed into me carefully.

I was glad that he was behind me and couldn't see my face. He couldn't see that I closed my eyes and allowed myself to surrender to his touch. I knew he liked to watch me come, but he was making it all about me that morning.

My back arched, pushing my ass further into his hard cock and unintentionally giving him better access. His finger stroked in and out of me and then he pulled out and pushed back into me with two fingers. I moaned and he responded by plunging into me faster and deeper. My hips made small circles, thrusting into his hand as he finger fucked me with the hands of a man that knew a woman's body.

I was panting and mindless and my knees began to buckle beneath me. Jack moved his hand at my breast to around my waist, taking a firm grip on me as he felt my body start to surrender to its weight. He was breathing heavy too as he spoke. "I have you, baby. Give in to it." His thumb moved to cover my clit and he rubbed in gently but firm circles.

My body tightened and I screamed out as I came while he pushed his fingers in and out of me over and over again in a steady rhythm.

Jack held me as I came down from my orgasm and then allowed my raised t-shirt to fall back down around me. He kissed the back of my neck lovingly and turned me around to face him, pulling me into a hug with my head pressed against his chest. I loved the feel of him holding me tenderly.

After a few minutes, he pulled back to look at me. "We still need to talk." His lips pressed to my forehead in a gentle kiss.

"But I didn't take care of you yet." My answer was sheepish.

"Feeling you come is taking care of me." Jack pushed a lock of hair behind my air tenderly.

"That's sweet, but it doesn't help with that." I looked down at the bulge in his pants and smiled.

He laughed lightheartedly and planted a chaste kiss on my lips. "True, if you still want to take care of me after we talk, then I'll let you." He held me tight and I had a sick feeling in my stomach that he knew it might be the last time he held me.

I decided to shower before we sat down to talk. I needed to clear my head after our morning interlude in the kitchen. Jack showered after me, while I did a half-ass job of blow drying my hair and threw on a little mascara. I watched in the reflection in the mirror as he came out of the bathroom wrapped in only a towel. I didn't think I would ever get used to how beautiful the man was. Everything about him was just so damn masculine and sexy. His body was worthy of worship and I knew that he worked hard at maintaining it. God just didn't make creatures look like that. Shit like that came from a lot of hours in the gym.

I was frozen in the mirror when he dropped the towel and pulled on the jeans from the night before without anything underneath. He still had a full erection and, oddly, I found it endearing that he hadn't taken care of it in the shower. I was so caught up in feasting on his body with my eyes that I didn't notice he was watching me watch him through the mirror. He lifted his arms over his head to put on his shirt and all of the muscles in his shoulders and pecks flexed. "If you keep looking at me like that, we aren't going to have that talk today." He pulled the shirt down over his flat stomach, obscuring my view of his sexy as hell happy trail.

Shit. He had caught me when my mouth had literally been hanging open. I was just glad that I wasn't actually drooling when I was caught. His sexy eyes were dark and I was certain he wanted me as bad as I wanted him. But I needed to have a clear head when we spoke and figure out what was going on between us. "Full of yourself aren't you?"

I watched as he walked up behind me in the mirror and put his hands on my shoulders. His eyes never left mine in the mirror as he leaned down to whisper in my ear. "I'd much rather be filling you, baby." His words sent a shiver down my spine and he knew my body reacted to him.

"Well, let's get this talk over with then, shall we?" I was teasing, but the smile vanished from his face. He was nervous about our talk and it made me scared of what I was about to hear.

We sat down in the living room. I curled my feet up underneath me on the couch and he sat across from me in the chair. "So do I get ten more questions?" I tried to break the tension in the room with a teasing question. He smiled but the smile didn't make it up to his eyes.

"What do you know about me and my work Syd?" His voice was serious.

"Well, I know that you own 51% of the Heston Hotel chain voting stock. You pointed that out to your father backstage last week."

"I do. My grandfather started the hotel chain and gave my father 49% when he was old enough to get involved in the business. Then when he died, he left 49% to me and 2% to my mother. We had all expected that my mother's will would leave both my father and I each 1% when she died, so that we would be equal partners, but she didn't. She left me the 2%, giving me controlling interest in the hotels. I didn't think she knew about my father's affairs when she was alive, but after her will was read I realized that she did."

Wow, there was a lot of screwed up information there, but that didn't sound like something that would send me running for the hills. "I take it your father wasn't happy about your having more control of the business then him?"

"My father doesn't like anyone but him to have any control."

Hmmm ... maybe there was more there than I thought. Did he realize that the apple didn't appear to fall far from the tree on the control issue? "Okay." I dragged the word out, letting him know that I was waiting for more.

"The hotels aren't my only business." He paused and looked into my eyes. "Do you remember me telling you that I invested in a business to embarrass my father?"

I shook my head, waiting for the rest.

"I own a production company." Jack ran his fingers through his hair and blew out a deep breath.

"Okay." My brows furrowed in confusion.

"I own the largest porn film production company in the United States, Syd. My other business is making porn."

He watched me intently, waiting for my reaction. My first thought was, *Okay, that isn't so bad.* But then memories of our past conversations came flooding back and I started to put together the pieces of the puzzle. *He had 500 to 1,000 partners. He is amazing in bed.* That women, with the over the top appearance at the conference, he said he'd brought her to piss off his father. *Was she an actress?* I felt the bile in my stomach rise to my throat and it stung as I opened my mouth to speak. "Have you ever been in one of the films?" I held my breath waiting for the answer.

"No." His response was immediate and unwavering.

"Have you been with any of the actresses?"

"Yes."

My heart clenched. "Was the woman that you were with last weekend at the conference an actress?"

"Yes."

"Is she your girlfriend? Were you with her after you got back from Hawaii?" The thought of him being with her after the week that we had shared made me sick. The tears filled my eyes and I looked away, fighting back their escape.

"No, I didn't lie to you. I haven't had a girlfriend since I was a teenager. And I wasn't with her after I got back from Hawaii."

He moved from the chair to sit next to me on the couch and I kept my head turned from him. I wanted to hide my emotions. He took my face in his hands and gently forced me to look at him. I saw pain in his eyes and the tears started flowing down my cheeks.

He looked into my eyes as he spoke. "Syd, I'm not proud of who I am or things that I have done. And I know I don't deserve you. You're sweet and good and everything that I'm not. I tried to keep away so you wouldn't get hurt, but I can't help myself when it comes to you. I never wanted to be with a woman the way I want to be with you. I want to lie under the stars with you and talk for hours, and walk in the park holding your hand. You make me feel like I can be a better man. I'm terrified of the things you make me feel and I don't know how to control it."

I buried my head in his chest and he wrapped his arms around me while my tears turned to sobs. I wasn't even sure why I was crying, I was just so wrought with emotions and everything he had shared that I couldn't help but explode. Jack stroked my head until I slowly calmed in his arms. He whispered, "You okay, baby?"

I nodded. "I just need to lay down for a bit. My head is pounding."

Jack pulled off his shirt and laid himself back on the couch, pulling me to his warm chest and wrapping me in his arms. Neither of us was running away, it was a start.

I had no idea how long I had slept, but my headache was gone when I woke up. And at least I didn't think I was going to throw up anymore. I looked up and found Jack awake, watching me.

He spoke softly and stroked my hair. "Hey."

"Did you sleep?" I stretched a bit and then snuggled closer into his chest.

"No."

"Are you okay?"

He shook his head and gently laughed. "I lay out all my fucked up dirty laundry at your feet and you ask me if *I'm* okay? And you wonder why I can't keep away from you."

He kissed my forehead. I sat up on the couch on my knees and straddled one leg on each side of him as he laid on his back. "If we are going to try this, there is no mixing business with pleasure for you. In fact, there is no pleasure for you with anyone but me." I punctuated the sentence with my finger into his chest.

"Deal. But you know I don't have much experience with relationships, so you need to have patience with me."

I smiled at him. "Patience, yes. Tolerance for cheating, no."

Jack moved and before I even knew what he was doing, he had switched our positions. I was on my back and he was kneeling on the couch above me, his legs straddled on either side of me.

"Got it, no cheating. And just so we are clear, you belong to me now, so no one touches your ass but me either."

My heart melted at the thought of belonging to Jack. "Deal."

Jack leaned down, bringing his face close to mine. "Are we done talking for now?"

I nodded. His handsome face so close to mine was a major distraction to my brain.

"Good, because, baby, I've been in this apartment for almost a day while your sweet little ass laid on top of me and squirmed with my fingers inside of you. If I don't bury myself inside of you within the next five minutes, you aren't going to be able to walk tomorrow."

My eyes opened wide at his words, then narrowed and squinted as if to test him to see if he was telling the truth.

His smile was wicked and sexy. "On the couch or in the bedroom, babe?"

Okay, so he wasn't kidding. My stomach did a flip and I took a deep breath and rolled my eyes, pretending it was a sacrifice. "Bedroom."

"Good girl." He scooped me up carried me into the bedroom.

For the first time since I moved to New York, I dreaded going to work. Jack and I had come so far in the last twenty-four hours and I hated that I had to leave him already. I wanted to stay in bed and snuggle with him all weekend. But I couldn't let the band down, and the club would be busy on a Saturday night, so I forced myself to get up and get ready. When I walked out dressed for work, Jack was talking on his cell phone. I watched as he slowly looked me up and down. I had purposely dressed in my favorite red shirt and black form-fitting skirt, pairing it will five inch stilettos and a dozen long silver chains in all different lengths.

He kept his eyes on me as he spoke into his phone. "I don't give a fuck what it costs, just do it." He snapped the phone shut and walked to me.

"Is that what you wear to work every night?"

I played dumb. "No, I don't wear this outfit to work every single night. I wear all different outfits, silly." I placed the palms of my hands against his chest. "Everything okay, you sounded pissed on your call?"

"Yes, everything is fine. It was hotel business." He wrapped one arm around my waist and tugged me against him hard. "Do you feel that, Syd? I just look at you dressed like that and I'm fucking hard again. How am I supposed to watch you go to work, knowing a room full of drunk men will feel the same way about my woman?"

Fuck. Me. His jealous streak excited me and now I was going to have to walk around all night with an aching between my legs. "I only want one man, sweetie." I reached up on my tippy toes to kiss his mouth softly.

Jack had insisted that he drop me at the hotel on his way home. A sleek black Mercedes SUV was parked out front when we got downstairs. I took one look at the car and knew it was Jack's. "Yours?" I looked at him and rolled my eyes in response to his smirk.

Jack navigated us with his hand at the small of my back to the SUV door and the driver jumped out to open it. The uniformed driver nodded to Jack. "Evening, Mr. Heston."

We pulled up outside of the hotel and I had expected that Jack was dropping me off and going back to his place, but he told his driver to come back for him in an hour and got out with me. I looked at him quizzically as he helped me out of the SUV. "I have a few things to take care of here, so I thought I'd kill two birds with one stone."

He took my hand and we made our way through the hotel's front door.

"Two?" I thought maybe I had missed something. What was the other thing?

Jack smiled an evil but sexy as hell smile. "Within five minutes of walking through the front lobby holding your hand, the entire staff will be buzzing. It will make you off limits and security will make it their business to keep a closer eye on you."

I stopped dead in my tracks in the middle of the lobby. "So you're essentially a dog pissing on his territory."

Jack tightened the hand he was holding and pulled me to him, wrapping the other arm firmly around my waist. "Yep. Is that a problem, babe?"

I opened my mouth to respond and Jack used it as an opportunity to cover my mouth with his and kiss me. It wasn't a sweet quick kiss, it was a demanding make my knees week and leave me breathless kiss. His tongue explored my mouth and licked at my lips, stopping to suck in my tongue. When he broke the kiss, he kept his face close to mine, and I was lightly panting. "That should do it baby." He looked around, apparently satisfied with himself.

I peered to one side of the room, and then the other. Jack was right, we had apparently gotten the attention of everyone in the room. "You're unbelievable."

He kissed me chastely before letting me go. "And don't you forget it, babe."

An hour later Jack came back to the empty club while I was finishing my set-up routine and said goodbye. "Your place or mine tonight?" He said it like there was never any question that we would be spending the night together again that night.

I smiled. "Yours, your bathroom is bigger than my apartment."

"I'll be back at midnight for you."

"That's not necessary, Jack. I can take a cab to your place."

He kissed me sweetly on the lips. "I want to."

I sighed. "Okay."

Chapter 16

Sunday morning we slept late and it was early afternoon before we got out of bed. Jack ordered room service and a pot of coffee for me. We sat at his dining room table that could sit fourteen and I wondered how much entertaining he did that he needed such a big table.

"Do you host a lot of parties?"

"Here? No. The only people that have ever been up here are my boys that you met in Hawaii, and they don't require a dining room table or hosting."

His statement peaked my interest. "So, the five hundred or thousand women that you have … *entertained*, none of them have been here?" I dragged out the word entertained because fucked just didn't seem appropriate at the dining room table.

I saw Jack's face growing uncomfortable. "No, there has never been another woman in my bed, Syd. You are the first woman I've *entertained* here." He drew out the word entertained the same as I did, mocking my choice of words.

My inner goddess was delighted with the news that no woman had been in his bed before. But something didn't make sense. "So where did you *entertain* the women then?"

Jack's jaw tensed and I instantly knew I wasn't going to like the answer. He looked down at his plate. "I keep a room on the fifteenth floor."

I almost choked on my coffee. "You keep a fuck room?" My voice was louder and more condescending than I meant it to be.

"I kept a room where I could spend the night, a small suite. I kept some of my things down there. It has an office in there too." His voice was controlled and I could tell he was trying to restrain his emotion and not be defensive.

"Do you have an office here too?" I wasn't trying to be sarcastic, but it came out that way anyway.

"I told you I wasn't proud of my past, Syd. But we're together now and you're in my bed, not in that room, so let's not do this." Jack got up from the table and stormed out of the room.

I sat for a few minutes, thinking. Jack was right. I was jealous and acting like a brat. He had been honest with me from the start and never pretended he was anything other than who he was. He didn't deserve my judgment. I cleared the table and went to apologize.

I found him in his exercise room, running full speed with headphones on. He watched me as I walked in, but didn't slow his pace or take out his headphones. I mouthed the words *I'm sorry* to him and he nodded his head as he ran. He was dripping from the insane pace that he was running at and his shirt was sticking to his heaving chest, outlining every cut of his gorgeous body. Jack kept running, but caught my eyes wandering around his body. I could tell that my admiration for his body had distracted him, but he appeared content to keep running.

I pulled off his big t-shirt that I was wearing and stood there before him, completely bare. His lust-filled eyes roamed all over my body, but still he didn't break pace. Then I slowly knelt down and looked up at him under hooded eyes. That was it. He pushed stop and was in front of me within seconds. I pulled down his pants, opened my throat, and gave him the best apology I knew how.

Sunday night we sat around reading the three different newspapers that Jack had delivered and I was in my glory. It felt so natural and easy that I couldn't believe we had only met a month ago. I hated to leave, but we had been together since Friday night and I was nervous it would be too much too fast. Besides, I had no clothes or toiletries with me and I definitely needed my birth control pills.

"I'm going to take a quick shower if you don't mind, and start to get ready to go." It felt awkward to say, but I wasn't sure why.

"But you don't have to be in work until tomorrow night?" More of a statement then a question.

"I know, but I don't have any clothes or things here."

"What do you need? I'll send Mateo to get whatever you need."

"Mateo?"

"My driver. He's paid to be on call and usually I'm running around. It will give him something to do."

"I need clothes and underwear, Jack. Is Mateo going to go into my apartment and rummage through my underwear drawer?"

"No. I'd have to break his fingers for touching your underwear. But I can send him to Barney's to pick up some items that Chloe picks out."

"Chloe?" Did this man have a person to do all of his errands?

"She picks out my clothes. I'll call her and she can pick out some things for you and Mateo can pick up the bags." He said it as if it was simple and normal to have people run out and get my underwear.

"That's sweet, Jack, but I'll just go home. You are probably getting sick of me anyway. I've been here all day and night."

Jack froze. "Are you sick of being with me, Syd?" For a second he looked vulnerable.

"No, of course not." I could see he needed reassurance. "It's just, I'm afraid of taking things too fast. I know you are new to relationships and I don't want to push you too fast and scare you away."

Jack's confident face returned as he grabbed his cell phone. "I spent three weeks torturing myself without you, babe. I'm not letting you slip away now that I have you."

My heart swelled a little more at his affirmation. He pushed a button on his cell and the conversation was over. He kissed my forehead as he walked out of the room talking on his phone. "Nope, not for me today, Chloe, I need you to put some things together for my girlfriend."

His girlfriend? I loved the sound of that.

Two hours later there was a knock at the door.

I heard Jack and Mateo talk for a minute, but I was only dressed in one of Jack's t-shirts so I didn't go out to see what Mateo had brought, even though I was curious. A few minutes later Jack came back to the living room. I was camped out on his area rug with newspaper sections spread all over the floor. He plopped a few bags down on the couch. "How about we go out to dinner tonight?"

"That sounds great." I motioned to the half dozen bags on the couch. "It looks like I have something to wear." I smiled and shook my head.

Jack walked to me and reached down to where I was sitting and kissed me on the forehead. Something about when he kissed me on the forehead made my insides melt. "As much as I'd really love to make you model all your new clothes for me, I have an hour or two of work that I have to get done. So why don't you go see if you can find something you like and I'll go to my office to work so that seeing your naked body won't distract me."

"Okay." Damn, he was cute when he was sweet.

"I'll bring the rest of the bags to the bedroom and make space in the closet for you to keep your things."

"The rest of the bags?" There were six on the couch. How many bags were delivered? And he was going to make me space in his closet? Holy shit.

"I told her to send over whatever would look sexy on your cute little ass. Apparently she Googled you and found pictures of you singing and there is a lot you will look sexy in." I was momentarily speechless, but it didn't matter, because Jack wasn't finished. "And we need to talk about Internet security, or lack of security. Any crazy man can find out where you live."

Umm ... yeah. You did.

Jack wasn't kidding when he said Chole had researched me. There were at least two dozen outfits and each one was something that I would have picked out for myself. That is, if I had about $50,000 to go on an insane shopping spree. There were bags and bags of beautiful shirts, pants, shoes, bras, underwear and even lingerie and a robe. Then there were cosmetic and hair products, all of which in the brands that I used. It was over the top, insane, and way too much. I stopped looking at the tags when I found a box of shoes that were marked $1,600 alone.

I decided to keep my favorite outfit, because I really didn't have anything to wear if I didn't, and the cosmetics and hair products. The rest was in a huge heap on the bed, and Jack was going to have to have Mateo take them back.

Jack finished in his office and came up behind me as I was getting ready. "Jack, there are way too many clothes there. I picked one outfit to wear tonight, but the rest need to go back. I appreciate you buying them for me, but it's way too much."

"Nope." He kissed the top of my forehead and lifted his shirt off. "I'm going to take a quick shower."

What? He'd dismissed everything I said in one little word and wasn't even going to wait around to discuss it with me? He really was going to need a lot of tutoring on how relationships worked. "Jack, don't ignore what I just said."

I looked up at him in the mirror behind me and saw his face looked annoyed. "I didn't ignore what you just said. I considered it and responded to it."

"You considered it and responded to it?" Was he insane?

"Yep. Give me three good reasons why you can't keep them and I'll change my mind. I'm not unreasonable."

I felt the heat in my face rise. Was he joking? I didn't even know how to respond to that statement. And god damn it, I was drawing a blank for three good reasons why I couldn't keep them.

His angry face changed to amused as he watched me in the mirror. "You got nothing, huh?" One eyebrow arched in challenge. "Do they fit?"

"Yes."

"Do you like them?"

"Yes, but that's not the point."

"So why don't you tell me what the point is then, Syd."

His rapid fire of questions was pissing me off. "It's too much, Jack. You just don't go around buying your girlfriend of two days $50,000 of clothes."

"You don't?"

I could tell in his voice he was screwing with me and it just made me madder. "No, you don't, it's too much, too soon."

"Why?"

God, he infuriated me. He infuriated me because I didn't have an answer. I didn't know why it was too much, too soon. It just was. "It just is, Jack."

He stepped out of the low hanging sweatpants that he was wearing as he spoke. "That's not an answer, Syd. You still haven't given me any good reasons, babe."

He was right, I hadn't given him any reasons, but that didn't mean that I was keeping the clothes. I gave him my best pissed off look in the mirror and he didn't flinch.

"Let's look at this another way, Syd. Would it be acceptable for a new boyfriend, who earns say $100,000 a year, to buy his new girlfriend a $500 outfit if he wanted to?"

I thought about it. Michael had earned only a little more than that and I guess I wouldn't have thought it was too much if he had bought me an outfit costing $500. "I guess not — it would be generous, but I wouldn't think it was insanity." Jack removed his boxer briefs and stood behind me with his glorious naked body. If I couldn't come up with an intelligent answer before he was naked, how the hell was I supposed to think with that staring at me in the mirror?

"Then it's all relative, babe. Just add a few zeros to the salary and I should be allowed to add a few zeros to what I spend on my girlfriend's clothes." And with that, Jack turned away and walked into the bathroom. I couldn't help but watch as every muscle in his fantastic ass tightened with each stride.

I thought about what Jack had said while I got dressed and I was glad for a few minutes to think about the conversation without the pressure of Jack's intense questioning. Was he right? I'd never dated a man that earned millions of dollars. Maybe it was all relative? But it still didn't sit right with me for some reason, even if I couldn't give him three good reasons why.

Jack came out of the bathroom wrapped in a towel and lord he was sexy. The towel hung low and showed off his deep v and that little light line of hair that lead from his belly button down to that place that made my stomach flip flop.

"How did you know what shampoo and conditioner and makeup brands I used?" It seemed like way too much of a coincidence that Chloe had happened to select all of my favorite brands.

Jack threw the towel on the bed and walked into his closet stark naked. I was pretty sure I would never get used to how beautiful the man looked without clothes on. "Sienna told Chloe what you used." His tone was matter of fact as if he was saying something that wouldn't shock me.

He stepped out of the closet pulling up the zipper on a pair of dark gray slacks.

"What? How did Sienna talk to Chloe?" I was thoroughly confused.

"I gave Chloe Sienna's number and she called her."

"But how did you get Sienna's number?" I didn't even think he knew Sienna's last name.

He pulled on a light blue dress shirt as he spoke. "I told you we were going to talk about Internet security, Syd. Any lunatic could find out anything he wanted about the two of you with a few keystrokes."

"I guess he did." I was exasperated. We were going to talk about Internet security? How about we talk about boundaries and stalking?

My comment didn't seem to faze Jack in the slightest; he continued to get ready without missing a beat. "Get dressed, babe, we're going to be late."

"Late for what?" I seemed to always be a step behind him in our conversations.

"Dinner. We have reservations at 8:30 at Coco LaMer."

Coco LaMer was the *it* place of the year. I had passed by it a few times on my way to work and once I saw two of the girls from *Sex in the City* going in for dinner. I heard the reservation wait was two months long, although I never bothered to verify that information because that type of restaurant wasn't in my budget. I didn't bother to ask how Jack got reservations. The man clearly got whatever he wanted.

I took my turn in Jack's walk-in closet and dressed in the outfit that I had chosen to keep. It was a gold-colored strapless dress. The top was made of a delicate lace that wrapped around me like strips of gauze, winding in different directions. The waist was high and had a large bow on the right side. The bottom was a shredded mess of sparkly gold strips that completely clashed with the delicate top. It looked like a walking piece of art and fit me perfectly. I paired it with the shoes Chloe had picked, five inch stiletto sandals that wrapped around my ankles. I had long lean legs, but the short skirt and high heels made my legs look crazy long.

I knew I looked good and I was glad that I had decided to leave my hair down. I walked out of the closet as Jack was clasping his watch on and his reaction was all that I had hoped for and more.

"Fuck, Syd. You look beautiful. Sexy as hell."

I twirled to show him the full outfit and smiled at him. "Thank you, the outfit is beautiful. Chloe has incredible taste."

He walked to stand in front of me and took both my hands. "You are going to get me killed, with my temper and the looks you are going to get." Jack was dead serious and I loved every word.

I rolled my eyes, telling him he was exaggerating, and planted a kiss on his mouth.

Of course, the maitre d' at Coco LeMer knew Jack by name. While it was nice to get service as soon as we walked in, the thought of Jack bringing some of his 1,000 other women to the restaurant dulled my spirits. Jack was already getting good at picking up on things that bothered me and whispered, "I've only ever brought business associates here," as we walked to the table. I thought it was sweet that he noticed the little things.

Sienna jumped up as we arrived at our table. "Surprise!"

I hugged her as if I hadn't seen her in years. I was happy to see her, but confused. "What are you doing here?"

Sienna looked at Jack and smiled. "I threatened to kill him if he hurt you and he invited me to dinner."

Yep, that sounded about right for Sienna. I hadn't filled her in on all that had happened since Jack came back a few days ago. The last time I saw her I had been a mess, crying over him. So much had happened and it felt like months had passed in the last week.

"I'm sorry, Sienna, I should have called you." I took her hand.

"I'm the one who owes Sienna the apology, Syd. I was a complete asshole to you and Sienna was just being a good friend. I wouldn't have wanted her to react any other way when I called."

Sienna smiled at me. "We need to celebrate, Syd. How about tequila for a change?" We both cracked up.

The food was incredible and Sienna and I were happy to let Jack order for us. A few men stopped by the table during dinner to say hello to Jack and he introduced us each time, calling me his girlfriend. I loved hearing him call me his.

Sienna told me about some potential gigs that she was working on for us and we told Jack stories of the worst gigs we had ever done. The bat mitzvah where I'd had the flu and threw up behind the stage in a bucket in between songs — only for the little boy who was the guest of honor to trip over a few minutes later and be forced to wear a vomit-covered suit the rest of the night. The rave in an abandoned warehouse in Boston that got out of control when a biker that was hitting on me didn't know when to quit, causing a full blown war between two biker gangs to erupt. I don't think Sienna noticed Jack's jaw tighten as she told the story about the biker guy, but I didn't miss it.

Jack didn't tell many stories about his past, but I wasn't sure if it was because he didn't want to share or because Sienna and I monopolized the conversation most of the evening. Either way, the three of us laughed most of the night and I was surprised that three hours had flown by. Sienna and I excused ourselves and went to the ladies room to freshen up. I gave her the seven minute catch up on all that had happened. "Well, if I didn't see you guys together tonight, I would probably have been concerned when you got around to telling me you were reunited. But, shit, Syd, that man is in love with you."

In love with me, was she crazy? "That's the tequila talking, Sienna. He is not in love with me. In lust, maybe. But we haven't known each other long enough to be in love."

Sienna took my face into her hands. "Sweetie, time has nothing to do with it. You wasted seven years with that asshole. That's a whole lot of time. Did you ever feel for Michael what you feel for Jack?"

I thought about the question but didn't respond. She smiled broadly. "Right, time doesn't mean shit."

When we got back to the table, Jack was talking with a silver-haired man with a young face and neither of them looked happy. I could see the tension on Jack's face that hadn't been there ten minutes earlier. "All okay?" I stood next to Jack and put my hand on his shoulder. Young Silver looked at my hand on Jack's shoulder and then did an obvious slow, leering gaze up and down my body. I watched the whole thing and the look made my stomach turn. Unfortunately, Jack didn't miss it either. Jack stood and got in Young Silver's face, and spoke quietly, but I still heard every word.

"You don't know what you're talking about. And get your fucking eyes off of her before I make it so you can't fucking see."

Young Silver snickered, but didn't look my way again before scurrying back to where he came from.

Sienna and I sat, but the mood had changed. "Are you okay, babe?" I asked, tentatively.

"Yep. Sorry about that. Why don't we get out of here."

Mateo was waiting when we walked outside. I was glad that Jack insisted on dropping Sienna at her building since it was late. Jack was polite, but quiet, and I could tell that whatever had been discussed between him and Young Silver was still bothering him. But I decided not to push him on the subject and instead held his hand and sat quietly the rest of the way back to the hotel.

Monday afternoon I finally went home. I was surprised to hear Michael's voice on my answering machine. His voice was low and full of remorse. He blabbered on about wanting to find out how I was doing and something about finding my grandmother's necklace. I pressed delete and didn't bother to call him back. I didn't want to be bitter about all those years I had spent with Michael, but the way it ended had left me feeling that I had lived with a man that I never really knew, a man I really didn't like.

As I got ready for work, I found myself thinking of Jack and what he was doing. He had said that he was going to work after dropping me at my apartment, but what did going to work entail for a man that was in his business? I had come home from Jack's on a high, feeling good about our new relationship, and less than two hours later I was questioning his intentions after just one message from Michael. It had taken me seven years to take off the blinders and see who Michael really was. I was afraid of making the same mistake again.

Chapter 17

The next week flew by and Jack and I were almost inseparable. I spent most of my time at his apartment when I wasn't working. After our first week together, he had insisted that Mateo would pick me up after work, and I knew that arguing a cab was just as safe was a losing battle. Each night Mateo was waiting outside when I walked out and he whisked me directly to Jack's hotel. We had started to settle into a routine where Jack would get up early to exercise and I would find him working in his home office when I crawled out of bed about 11. He always seemed to finish up whatever he was working on when I came into his office, and I wasn't sure if it was sweet or he didn't want me to look at what he was doing.

I was excited when Jack invited me to a business dinner. There was such a big part of him that I didn't know and I thought that perhaps seeing him at work would quell that little nagging feeling in the back of my head that kept me always searching for signs of a different man than who I was hopelessly starting to fall for.

I dressed for the dinner in a simple cream pencil skirt, rose colored silk blouse, and nude sling backs. I decided to pull my normally loose falling blonde hair back into a slick ponytail for a more demure look. I must have achieved the look I was going for, because when Jack saw me he told me he had the urge to fuck me hard in between the stacks at the library.

Dinner turned out to be with an older gentleman who brought a woman that I initially thought was his daughter, but who turned out to be his wife. The restaurant was packed with businessmen and a few women, most of whom eyed Jack as he passed. I didn't blame them; Jack was a sight in his navy sports jacket with light tan pants and simple striped tie. Aside from being devastatingly handsome, Jack carried himself with such confidence it exuded masculinity from him that made women swoon.

Jack and I maintained a physical connection throughout the meal. We either held hands, or he leaned his leg against mine or rested his arm around the back of my chair. It made me wonder if he was aware of the women that looked his way and it was his unspoken way of comforting me, or if he had caught the guy at the table closest to us looking my way, as I had earlier.

Either way, I thought it was sweet and his touch on me just seemed so natural.

It turned out that our dinner guest owned a small chain of hotels in Illinois and Jack had been researching the properties as potential purchases. The Heston hotel chain had two properties in Chicago, but none in the outer cities, which apparently were good investments as the population was growing in the smaller, outlying cities.

Jack discussed what his engineers had found, and while I thought it was all very interesting, I was mildly disappointed that the business dinner was hotel related. I was curious about the other side of Jack's business and I had secretly hoped that the lunch would give me insight into that part of Jack's life.

After dinner we headed back to Jack's penthouse. Traffic was gnarled for a few blocks, and by the time we arrived I only had twenty minutes to change or I would be late for work.

Jack and I changed together in his closet, where I had left my outfit for the night.

"Thank you for coming to dinner with me. I hope you weren't bored too much?"

"No, it was nice, I was glad to come." I thought for a minute. He had given me an opening and I needed to take it if I was ever going to satisfy my curiosity on the other side of his life. "Although I have to admit, I was a little disappointed it was hotel business. You never mention your *other* business." I emphasized the word other, as if he wouldn't have known what business I was talking about without my doing so.

Jack stood silent for a minute and then came up behind me as I was letting down my hair. "You want to know more about my other business?"

I felt my face flush and was I glad that he was behind me. I don't know why it embarrassed me to admit that I wanted to know more, but I did. "Yes, I do. You didn't even want to tell me about that side of your life, so I think it has me curious."

Jack's arms wrapped around my waist and his face nuzzled in my hair. "Okay then, I'll bring you to my office with me one day if that will make you feel better."

I felt a flood of relief from a place I didn't even know was stressed. I turned to face him. "You will?"

Jack kissed me, a sweet, tender kiss on the lips before answering. "Whatever you want is yours, babe."

I smiled and kissed him chastely with excitement.

"Two conditions, babe."

Damn it, I knew that had been too easy. I looked up at him expectedly, waiting for the other shoe to fall.

"One: you remember it is a business for me and not part of my personal life."

"Okay. I can do that. What's the other condition?"

"You put your hair back in that ponytail and put on that naughty librarian outfit again when you get home tonight."

My insides melted a little bit, and it had nothing to do with him wanting me to play naughty librarian with him. Jack had called me coming to his penthouse, "coming home". It was exactly what it was starting to feel like, although it was the man and not the place that made it feel like home.

I reached up on my tippy toes and gave him a long, sultry kiss that said *I want to fuck you.* I sucked in his tongue and nibbled on his lip, but broke the kiss before I was unable to stop.

Jack leaned his forehead against mine. "Fuck, Syd." He pressed his obvious erection into me. "The librarian is going to get a spanking tonight for leaving me like this."

I knew it wasn't nice to do, but I loved leaving him wanting more of me. I felt empowered by the effect I had on Jack, who seemed so unaffected by everything else in his life.

An hour into our performance, I spotted Lyle come into the club. He waited until the end of our first set and then huddled us together whispering as if he were about to let us in on classified government secrets. "There have been some reports of a rat being in the club today. We are closing down two hours early for the exterminators to treat the entire floor." I immediately started scanning the room to look for the creature and suddenly had the urge to get back up on the raised stage. Lyle went on that the patrons would be offered free drinks to move to the lobby bar at closing, but that we were free to go early and would be paid for the full night.

Although the thought of a rat in the same room as me made my head spin, the early evening was a welcome surprise, and I decided to take a cab over to Jack's to surprise him. But when I went out front to hail a cab, I found Mateo waiting for me. I walked to the car and, as usual, he jumped out to open my door. "Good evening, Ms. St. Claire."

"Hi Mateo. How did you know I was getting out early?"

Mateo seemed confused by the question. "Jack called to tell me to pick you up at 10."

I climbed in the car and sat thinking. How did Jack know that I was getting out early? I knew he owned the hotel, but did they really bother him with every little thing that went on in the hotel? It seemed odd for a man who owned a chain of hotels to be aware of a club closing a few hours early.

The doors opened to the penthouse and I found Jack standing in the kitchen pouring two glasses of wine. He handed me a glass in exchange for a kiss and I kicked off my shoes as I spoke. "How did Mateo know that I was getting off early tonight?"

Jack looked at me with a sheepish, but devilish grin. "You left with some unfinished business." He sipped from his glass, his eyes watching me intently as he drank.

It took me a second to connect the dots, but then I

gaped at him with my mouth hanging open. "Are you saying what I think you are saying?"

"I don't know. What do you think I'm saying?" He smirked, actually smirked, at me!

"You had them close down the club just to get me home two hours early to have sex with you?"

Jack clanked his wine glass down on the counter and took mine from my hand as I was about to take a sip. "You have no fucking idea what lengths I would go to have sex with you." Then he picked me up and threw me over his shoulder caveman style and carried me to the bedroom.

Chapter 18

Almost a week went by before Jack asked me if wanted to come to his *other* office. I was starting to think that he had forgotten, and a strange part of me almost hoped that he had. I wanted to pretend that the other part of him didn't exist. I was blissfully happy with my Jack, the hot hotelier that I had become inseparable from. The thought of seeing another side to him, one that had the potential to change who he was to me, was physically painful to me.

I was surprised when we pulled up at a nondescript building that I had passed many times but never actually noticed. I'm not sure what I had expected, but flashing neon signs with a large XXX would have fit what my wild imagination had envisioned better.

The lobby was typical office-building-gray and there was a central desk with a security guard who greeted Jack by name when we entered. I still hadn't said a word as we entered the elevator and Jack pushed the button for the third floor.

"Is just your office on the third floor or do you share space with other companies?" I was forcing myself to make small talk to keep my heart from pounding out of my chest.

"I own the building. Cole Productions occupies the entire space."

Cole Productions, it sounds so businesslike; definitely better than Jerkoff Jack's I suppose. And his business occupies the entire building? If there were no other companies in the building then I would have expected there to be half naked girls making out in the hallway or something.

We approached a door and I started to panic. My heart raced and I was sure Jack could feel the sweat in my palms. Jack stopped at the door and turned to me. I must have looked as bad as I felt, because I saw the panic written on his face. "Are you okay, babe?"

"Yes," I lied.

"Are you sure you want to do this? I've been sick the last week thinking of bringing you here. You are so good and sweet and everything I'm not, and I don't want to taint you with my disgusting life." He held my face in his hands and wiped away a stray piece of hair.

I put my hands on his and didn't expect what I said next to come rolling off my tongue. "I don't want to come, but I have to. I need to know who you are and this is a big part of you. I can't let myself fall in love with a man who has another side that I've never seen."

"Fuck, babe. That's what I love about you: pure and honest, no games." He kissed my lips gently and pulled me close to whisper in my ear. "I'm falling in love with you too, babe."

Holy. Shit. We picked a fine place for a heart to heart. The door we were standing in front of abruptly opened and the momentary swell of love in my heart was pierced by a silver bullet as I stared into the face of the woman who Jack had brought to the conference what seemed like a long time ago.

"Jack, baby, it's about time. We have two live shoots today, a cover to pick, and the writers want approval on the final script in the *Candy* series." She put her long red fingernails on his arm and I immediately wanted to scratch out her eyes.

"Jenna, this is Sydney. Give us about fifteen minutes to settle in and I'll start with the cover."

Jenna gave me a fake smile and I gave her one back. I'd seen the woman twice and heard her speak once, and I was damn certain that she wanted Jack. Or worse, had already had him.

Jenna walked off and Jack took my hand and squeezed it tightly before leading the way to his office. The walk down the halls to his office gave the first glimpse that the office was anything more than a typical office. There were framed posters and awards, much of which would have seemed normal in a movie production company — if the people in the posters had been wearing clothes. I tried not to gawk as we walked, but I couldn't help myself.

Jack's office was nothing like the hall and nothing like I expected. If was big and clean and there were no signs of either porn or his personal life. "Did you clean out your office for my visit, or does it always look so empty and sterile?"

Jack laughed. "Nope, this is how it always is. I take it you expected something different?"

I shook my head, embarrassed.

"Like I told you, Syd. This started out as nothing more than something to embarrass my father. Then it turned into a profitable business. It's a business to me. One I actually like running, unlike the hotels which scream of my father at every turn. I don't keep pictures on the wall or films all over, because I keep it strictly business in here. And you're the only woman I've ever wanted to look at while I was working, so I guess I'll have to break the sterility and get a framed picture of you for my desk soon."

I rolled my eyes at him, but the thought of him only having a picture of me in his stark office did warm my heart. "So am I going to get a day in the life of Jack Cole Heston view today?"

"We should talk about that before I start the day, babe. There are shoots going on here and I usually go check them out. I can go check in and you can hang out in here if that makes you feel more comfortable."

His offer was thoughtful, but I wanted to see it all: the good, the bad, and the ugly. "I want the full tour, you don't need to leave me behind."

Jack eyed me tentatively and I could tell he was considering his response carefully. His eyes caught mine, searching for something. He blew out a deep breath. "Okay."

Our first business of the day was script approval. We met with the two men and a woman who were the writing team for the multi-partner movies. I was surprised to find a woman writer and even more surprised at how businesslike and professional the meeting was. They skipped over the sex scenes and just spoke about the storyline. I wasn't a virgin to X-rated movies, but I must have watched the wrong ones, because none of the movies that I'd watched seemed to have had an actual realistic story like the ones we reviewed that day.

After script approval we moved onto covers. We met with a photographer, who showed Jack and I a bunch of glossy photos for a movie called Triple Double, which apparently referred to triplets who starred in movies together and all had double D breasts. The photographer was a nice older man, maybe in his late sixties. It was odd to hear the man talk about his grandchildren while they were looking at glossies of women holding themselves open with one hand and inserting a vibrator with the other. But it really did seem like a business and not the wild orgy I had imagined.

Our last stop of the morning was a visit to the set to check in on the progress of two movies. I wasn't nearly as nervous as I was when we'd first arrived, after seeing how professionally things were run. Jack's assistant came by and took our lunch order and then we headed down to what Jack called "the hanger." The hanger was the entire basement of the building that was split into two extremely large spaces, each set up to accommodate many sets.

Jenna met us at the door and I cringed when she put her hand on Jack's arm as she spoke.

"Set 2 is vanilla. It might be the better one for you to take your friend on her tour."

God, I hated that woman. She needed to get her fucking hands off of Jack and stop speaking about me as if I wasn't standing right there. I didn't want to come across as a jealous crazy person, but I couldn't let her get away with it. "Since we had vanilla at home this morning, why don't we try Set 1, honey?"

Jack's eyebrows shot up, and then I saw a glimmer of a smirk. He looked proud of my response. Before Jack could respond, the door to Set 1 opened and a man walked out.

"Hey, Mr. Cole, I'm glad you made it. We're just taking a ten minute break while they change into leathers. I have a few chairs set up to the left of my cameras whenever you are ready."

"Perfect, I actually need five minutes to make a call, so I'll see you inside in a few, Frank." Jack turned to face me. "I'm going to run upstairs for a few minutes to make a quick call. We can't get service down here. You want to come or wait down here, babe?"

"Actually, I saw a ladies room down the hall. Why don't I meet you back here after your call?"

Jack nodded and planted a quick kiss on my lips before disappearing down the hall.

I didn't give any thought to the sound of the door opening in the ladies room. I used the bathroom and exited the stall to find Jenna leaning with her back against the sinks, waiting for me. I pretended her presence didn't faze me and stood next to her in silence as I washed my hands, looking at her back in the mirror.

"A word of advice, woman to woman. Don't get too attached, Jack will get bored of you soon. He always does. He'll wine you and dine you and take you to his love nest in that fancy hotel of his for a week or two, then he'll move on to the next plaything."

I felt bile burning my throat. I had suspected that Jenna wanted something from Jack, I just hadn't been sure if it was business or personal. Her words confirmed that she wanted more from him than he had given her, but the thought of her being in Jack's love nest room made me physically sick. I had to grip the sides of the sink to hold myself steady. It took everything I had to plaster a smile on my face, but I knew I needed to deliver my message strong. *Ready, aim, fire!*

"He told me he used to take his concubines to a room on the 153rd floor. I've never seen it, though, we spend most nights in his penthouse or my apartment." Score! I watched her vicious smile fade and went in for the kill. "And, by the way, he's giving his *girlfriend* a tour, not his friend." I stressed the word girlfriend to get my point across. Then I dried my hands and held my head high as I walked out of the bathroom, leaving the bitch no chance to respond.

Jack was waiting for me outside the set, when I got back. He had become so good at reading me quickly. "Everything okay?" He looked at me, concerned.

Just as I opened my mouth to respond, Jenna passed without a word and went into the set. "Yes, everything is fine." I knew I didn't sound that convincing, because I wasn't that convinced I was fine either.

He eyed Jenna out of the corner of his eye as she passed and then looked back into my eyes, waiting for more, but I didn't add anything. "We'll talk about it later." He knew the conversation wasn't over, but I was glad he didn't plan to have it right there and then.

He kissed me on the lips gently. "Ready?"

"As I'll ever be."

The scene hadn't started yet, so we took our seats near the cameramen and I watched the set, fascinated by all the activity. I heard Jack speak to the guy setting up the cameras next to him, but my brain couldn't capture the words.

Two men were working on buckling and securing various black leather straps and chains crisscrossing a woman's naked body. Two makeup artists hurried to apply makeup, one painting bright red lipstick on the brunette's pale face, the other applying some sort of liquid to her ass-cheeks that were protruding between leather straps wrapped around each thigh, up the crack of her ass and wrapping around her lower back.

The chains and straps on her front wrapped around her exposed breasts in a similar pattern, and a loose silver chain hung from clamps attached to her nipples. The woman was attractive, but was made more striking by the contrast of the leather to her pale while skin. When the makeup crew was done, the men pulled at various chains until they were satisfied they were secure. Two men rolled in a workbench and placed what looked like normal carpenter's tools around the table. Then I watched as they secured the tools by hammering them into place on the table.

When they were done with the table, the leather-clad woman walked to it and dutifully leaned over it with her hands behind her back. The set guys then secured her wrists with leather cuffs and bound them together behind her tightly. A heavy chain slowly cranked down from the ceiling that I hadn't noticed was there before and then they clamped a hook into the back of the chains wrapped around her waist. They spent a few minutes ratcheting the chain until it was pulled taut and the women's ass was forced slightly in the air, positioning her heart-shaped ass to an angle that satisfied the camera man. The last crewmen wrapped a thick red silk scarf around the woman's eyes and everyone seemed pleased with the results.

Someone yelled and a handsome man appeared in a bathrobe. A woman brought him a hardhat and he handed her his robe, seemingly undaunted by the fact that he was standing with a massive erection in a room full of people. The director walked over and spoke to the two actors for a few minutes and my eyes were glued to the man gently stroking himself as if it was normal to stroke an erection while having a conversation with a fully clothed man and a blindfolded woman shackled to a table.

Finally the director and cameramen took their places and a woman handed the actor a black leather paddle. It looked as though the scene was about to start.

Jack had been holding my hand since we'd entered the room, but he squeezed to get my attention. I looked at him and he silently asked if I was okay and I nodded in response. I was glad that he wasn't expecting me to speak, because I was pretty sure I couldn't form words.

Just as I had seen on television hundreds of times before, someone yelled, "Quiet on the set," and a minute later, "Action!"

The naked man walked around the table and lowered his face to the blindfolded woman. "What's the punishment for being disobedient, Faith?

"Six paddles, Master."

"That's right. And you will not cum tonight. If you cum without my permission, the punishment will be much harsher. Do you understand me, Faith?"

"Yes, Master."

Master slowly circled around to the back of the table and stood behind Faith. He reached out and put both hands on her perfect ass and gently caressed for a minute. Then he took a step back with the paddle in his hand and a moment later the black leather paddle connected loudly with her ass. Faith gasped but said nothing. Instantly her right ass cheek reddened. Master moved closer and gently rubbed the right check. Then he knelt down and licked the other cheek slowly from top to bottom until her left cheek glistened. I felt a swell between my legs that surprised me.

Master stood again and pulled back his arm and an even louder smack sounded as the paddle connected with her wet cheek. Faith gasped again and then let out a low moan.

Master rubbed the left cheek and then stepped back again. He positioned his long erection in his hands and stroked up and down firmly a few times. Then he took one step forward and rammed himself straight into Faith without warning. He stayed planted to the hilt for a minute and then slowly circled his hips round and round. Another small moan escaped from Faith's mouth and Master pulled halfway out and then slammed in and out twice more before pulling all the way out.

Jack squeezed my hand I turned my head to find him watching me. For a split second I was embarrassed that I was visibly aroused, but then I heard another loud smack and I forgot everything else except for the couple in front of me. Master continued his punishment with another round of alternating smacks and licks and after the fifth paddle Faith's ass was bright red and I would have sworn the color on her ass matched my face. I was completely turned on and couldn't tear my gaze away as

Master finished the sixth paddle and again positioned himself behind Faith's ass, ramming into her with one deep long plunge, then slamming in and out of her relentlessly until he earned a high-pitched squeal; then he abruptly pulled out once more and circled the table in search of Faith's mouth.

I forgot where I was as I watched Faith hungrily swallow her Master's long hard cock and he punishingly fucked her mouth until he erupted in a ferocious growl and pulled out just in time for us to watch as he emptied himself all over her face and into her hungry, wanting mouth. For a moment I forgot that I was watching a live movie being filmed, until someone yelled, "cut," and people quickly scurried onto the set.

I forced myself out of my daze and looked over at Jack, hoping he hadn't noticed how transfixed I had become. No such luck. Jack was watching me like a hawk. In fact, I was pretty sure from looking at him that he had been watching me for a while. At first I couldn't bring myself to look into Jack's eyes. The haze of my arousal was lifting and embarrassment was seeping in. But I forced my eyes to his and found his pale green eyes dark with desire. "My office. Now."

Oh geez, what had I done? I had forced him to bring me there and now I had embarrassed myself. Jack said a few curt words to the director and took my hand, leading me out of the set and into the waiting elevator. He stood behind me and tightened his grip on my hand as the doors closed. "I've never seen anything so incredible in my life. " His voice was low and husky. I felt the need to respond, but couldn't. Luckily the elevator moved fast.

Jack led me to his office in a fury, never letting go of my hand. Inside, he pulled me around the front of his desk and lifted me so that I was sitting on the edge. "Watching you get aroused watching them was fucking torture. You are so fucking beautiful and I need to be inside you right this minute." Jack pushed my skirt up and ripped my panties from my body in one fluid movement.

He freed his massive erection and speared himself into me with such carnal desperation that I almost orgasmed before he even began to move. I was soaked with arousal and he growled as he pumped ferociously in and out of me. I knew how he felt; being inside me was something he desperately needed more than the air we breathed. I felt the exact same way.

Jack pulled his face back to look at me, never breaking his hasty rhythm. "I need to watch you. Come for me, baby."

His words were all I needed. It took less than five minutes for us both to spiral out of control and I felt his thick cum rush inside of me, throwing me deeper and harder into orgasmic bliss.

Jack held me as we fell to the floor together, breathless and panting. I had never cum so hard or so fast before and my body twitched as it sought to regain its control.

Even though Jack's penthouse was only a twenty minute drive away, I fell asleep in the car on the trip home. The entire day was swirling around in my head and I was emotionally and physically exhausted. I woke as Jack picked me up out of the car in the underground garage and carried me to the elevator. Normally, I wouldn't have been comfortable with being carried, but Jack made it seem like he was carrying feathers and I was too exhausted to argue with him. Instead, I wrapped my arms around his neck and snuggled into his chest.

The next morning I woke up and found Jack where I normally found him, busy at work in his office. He was on the phone, but didn't take his eyes off of me as I stood in the doorway. He motioned for me to sit on his lap as he spoke and I dutifully complied.

"Yes, go ahead, I'm fine with that. See if you can get him down ten, but go with it either way. Listen, I have something important that just fell into my lap that I need to deal with, so call me after it's done."

I smiled innocently and pointed to myself, pretending to be unsure if I was that something important that just fell into his lap.

His eyes never left mine as he nodded. "Whatever, I don't really care right now. Just deal with it." He hung up.

I swung one leg over him so that I was straddling him, my feet dangling from the chair. "Good morning," I swooned coyly.

"Sleep good?" Jack kissed my forehead.

I nodded.

"Good. We should talk about yesterday." Jack's business voice was back.

"Okaaay," I said clearly tentative on the topic.

"Are you okay with everything?" His voice was softer.

"I think so." I wasn't lying, I thought I was, but I hadn't allowed myself to really process the whole day. I needed time to really think about it all before I knew if I was okay with it all.

"Do you have any questions you want me to answer?"

Probably tons of them, but all except one escaped me that moment. "Did you sleep with Jenna?"

I saw Jack's jaw tense and I knew the answer before he even spoke. "Yes. But it was a long time ago. It didn't mean anything. There's been nobody since I met you."

"Nobody since you met me in Hawaii, or nobody since we got back together?" I was thoroughly surprised by his answer.

His answer was fast. "Nobody since I met you in Hawaii."

My heart fluttered in my chest at his response. I wanted to end the conversation and forget everything else existed. But I needed to know more. "She still wants you." A statement, not a question.

"No, we are just friends and she works for me."

Did he really not see that she wanted him? "She wants you."

"She's just protective and has an aggressive personality."

That's putting it lightly. "What does she do for you?" A loaded question.

"She's my sales manager. She sells the films into large chains and manages the sales team."

"Oh." His response surprised me. With her over the top sultry sex kitten appearance, I'd thought she was in films.

Jack knew exactly what I was thinking from my response. "She was in films. She retired and works behind the scenes now."

She couldn't be more than thirty. "Retired? So young?"

"She probably did sixty or seventy films. She's a legend in the business."

I felt my stomach turn. That was more than I needed to know. Immediately I felt insecure and nervous. I knew Jack had been with a lot of women, but I hadn't let myself think of the level of expertise that the women he had been with had. My only experience before Jack was Michael. I must have seemed inexperienced and awkward to Jack.

The man truly could read my mind. He gently pushed my hair behind my ear and lifted my chin to force me to look him in the eyes. "No one has ever made me feel like you do, Syd. There is no comparison, so get that shit out of your mind. Now."

"How do you do that?"

"Do what?"

"Know what I'm thinking all the time."

"It's important to me, so I pay attention." He wrapped his arms around my waist.

There was no way to respond to that, so I decided to hug him tight instead. To show him how important he was to me too.

Chapter 19

I had really thought I was okay with all that I'd learned about Jack's business for a few days. Then I went back to my apartment by myself and had a chance to really think about it. I had fooled myself into thinking it wasn't a big deal and that I could move forward. But it only took a half day away from Jack and another voicemail on my answering machine from Michael for my head to start spinning.

I remembered how aroused I had been watching the couple act out their scene at Jack's office. We had both exploded with such carnal need that we'd practically ran to find privacy so we could satisfy our craving. What happens when I am not there? I remembered the way the women all looked at Jack, like they wanted to eat him alive, especially Jenna. It would be so easy for him to have whoever he wanted, a woman with experience who knew how to satisfy a man. Being with me hadn't even been enough for Michael, and he didn't have porn stars available at his beck and call.

For the first time since I met him, I was glad that Jack was gone on a business trip and wouldn't be back until the next night. I needed some time to think and clear my head. Being around him just made everything seem so easy and natural, like it was just him and me against the world, and no one else existed. But that wasn't reality. I had walked around with blinders on for a long time with Michael, and I couldn't allow myself to be blind again. It hurt too much when it ended.

I sorted through my mail, exchanged a few texts with Sienna, and decided to call my mom before I had to get ready for work. She had left me another message a few days ago, but I was at Jack's and had completely forgotten to call her back. We talked for a while about her book club, Dad's latest wood project, and how I was adjusting in the city. I hadn't planned on mentioning Jack, because I didn't want to worry her. I knew she had been worried about me after my breakup with Michael, and I figured it was better not to mention that I was spending almost all of my free time with a man that she would assume was a rebound.

"I was starting to think I was going to have to send out a search party for you, dear."

"I'm sorry, Mom, I was out and didn't pick up the message until this morning." Half a lie was better than a full lie.

"I called three days ago. Were you traveling for a show?" Damn it, I had forgotten that Mom didn't miss anything. I needed to be more careful.

"Ummm, no. I was at a friend's."

"Siennas?"

"Ummm, no." Why couldn't I be a better liar? Some people didn't even have to think of a lie, they just opened their mouths and lies came out fluently.

"Did you make some new friends?" Crap. She wasn't going to stop until she got an explanation.

"No, Mom. I met someone. I wasn't going to mention it because it is so new." If you counted Hawaii, it had been almost two months already, so new wasn't exactly the truth.

"Oh." I knew how my mother worked. When she wanted more information, she would say, "Oh." And me, being the type of person I was, would not be able to take the awkward silence that ensued and would vomit an explanation. But I wasn't planning to give on the subject of Jack.

"Yes, Mom. I just don't want to talk about it yet."

"Oh."

Damn her. "I don't want you to worry about me, Mom. I'm fine."

"So I should be worried about the new man you are seeing?"

Yes, Mom, he makes pornos and has control issues. "No, Mom, I didn't mean that you should worry."

"Oh."

God damn it, I needed to get out myself out of her web.

"What I meant was, I knew you would worry about

me being in a relationship so soon after what happened with Michael."

"Of course I worry about you, honey, that's what mom's are supposed to do. So it's more than dating then? You're in a relationship?"

Shit, now I'd worried her and put her into full on interrogation mode. I had no choice but to tell her something to make her feel better.

"Yes, Mom. His name is Jack and he is very good to me." I breathed out a sign of relief as I finally spoke the truth.

"Where did you meet him?"

Shit, shit. I was completely unprepared for that one. "I met him at work, Mom." I was too mortified to tell my mother than I'd met a man on what was supposed to be my honeymoon.

"Oh, so you work with him?"

From the frying pan to the fire. "Sort of. Look, Mom, my doorbell just buzzed. I have to run."

"Okay, but I am thinking of coming down for a weekend. Maybe next weekend?"

Oh God, what have I done? "Sure, mom. Call me during the week. I have to run."

I kicked myself as I got ready for work for not being better prepared for my call with my mom. I had her worried and was going to be subjected to grueling in-person interrogation.

The night went by fast and the club was pretty quiet for a Thursday. It was almost midnight and we were on our final song when I caught him staring at me from his seat at the bar. Michael. What the hell was the asshole doing at the club? I looked away, but it was too late, he knew that I saw him. I finished up and he wasted no time in making his way to the stage.

"Why are you here?" I wasn't even going to pretend to be courteous.

"I needed to speak to you and you won't return my calls, Syd." Michael took a step toward me and I took one back. I knew Travis was at my side before I actually saw him just from the look on Michael's face.

"It's okay, Travis, I know him. But thank you." I smiled wearily at Travis to reassure him.

I saw a look of relief on Michael's face as Travis nodded and walked back to start packing up. "What do you want, Michael? Why do you keep calling me? " My voice was low to keep Travis under control, but I made no attempt to conceal that I was angry.

"Can we talk?" A pause as he searched my face for something. "Please?"

I exhaled loudly. "Fine, but I have pack up, so you can wait."

Michael nodded and went to wait by the bar.

I took my time packing up and had to reassure Travis I was okay three more times before he would leave. There were still a few stragglers in the club, so at least I wouldn't have to be alone with Michael.

Eventually I walked over to the bar, even though I dreaded looking at Michael, no less having a conversation in my place of work with him.

"Do you want a shot of tequila?" It annoyed me that he knew that I did, but I refused to give him the satisfaction of knowing how well he knew me.

"No." I stood a few feet from him as he sat on the bar stool.

"Can we sit at a table so that we have privacy? Please?" Michael looked to the bartender standing a few feet away and back to me.

I walked to an empty table a few feet from the bar and sat without saying a word, leaving him to follow me like a puppy.

Michael sat and I stared at him, waiting for the reason he was in New York, the reason he was at my job. He looked uncomfortable as he sat there looking back at me. He reached for my hand as he spoke. "Syd, I don't know where to start. I'm so sorry and I need you."

I pulled my hand away from his like it had burned me. I was suddenly past angry, closer to irate. I stood and spoke loudly "Is that why you came here?"

Michael jumped from his seat and reached out to grab my arm. "Syd, talk to me. You know—"

"Get your fucking hands off of her!" I heard Jack's voce before I even saw him.

Michael turned toward the voice and didn't see it coming. Jack's fist collided with Michael's cheekbone and I heard a loud crack. Michael fell onto the table and struggled to regain his footing.

"What the hell?" Michael mumbled as he stood holding his cheek.

Jack's arm reached out and pulled me behind him as he took a step closer into Michael's face. "It didn't look like she wanted you touching her."

Michael looked to me, confused. "Syd, who is this guy?"

The whole thing happened so fast, I just stood there looking at Michael.

"Babe, are you okay?" Jack's voice was softer when he spoke to me, but the anger was still there.

"I'm okay, he didn't hurt me."

"Babe? Who is this guy, Syd?" Michael's voice was angry. Did the asshole really think he could show up to my job to apologize after what he did to me and then get jealous and angry?

"He's my boyfriend, Michael, as if it was any of your business!"

"Michael?" Jack looked to me for confirmation if it was that Michael. I just nodded my head.

I didn't expect Jack to be happy to have met Michael, but I also didn't expect him to haul off and punch him again. The second punch landed on Michael's nose and blood flew everywhere.

Security surrounded us — not that Jack needed any help. "Are you okay, Mr. Heston?"

"I'm fine. Why wasn't someone here to keep an eye on Syd?"

The security team scrambled for an excuse. "Ummm ... she finished playing and the club was almost empty and we were changing shifts...."

Jack didn't give them time to finish. "Get this asshole out of here and be in my office at 7am. I'm not dealing with this tonight."

"Yes sir." The three security guards helped Michael to his feet and for a second I felt bad for him.

Jack grabbed my hand and took two steps toward the door before realizing I was still standing there. "Syd. Let's go." His voice brought me back to reality and I took one last look at Michael before I started to walk hand in hand with Jack to the door.

Mateo was waiting outside and I didn't say a word until we were halfway to Jack's. Then I remembered why I had been confused to see Jack. "I thought you were out of town until tomorrow?"

"Is that why you were with him, Syd?" Jack turned to face me; his face was masked and unreadable.

"What? No. I didn't even know he was coming, he just showed up."

"I came back because I didn't want to sleep without you next to me." Jack said it like he was laughing at himself even saying it, no less feeling that way.

I didn't know what to say. His words were so sweet, but the tone they were spoken in contradicted their meaning. "You don't believe me?"

"I don't know what to think, Syd. I walked in and saw that asshole touching you and I lost it. Then I saw your face, and him reach for you, and I wanted to kill him."

"I'm sorry, Jack." I reached for his hand and saw his swollen and bruised knuckles for the first time.

Jack turned to me, "What are you sorry for, Syd?"

"I'm sorry that he showed up. I'm sorry that it's my fault that you hurt your hand." I spoke each word into his eyes and watched as his eyes softened and I knew he believed me.

"It's not your fault."

Jack stood in his kitchen, his back against the island countertop, legs crossed at the ankle, arms folded across his chest, watching me put together an ice pack. I stood in front of him silently waiting for him to give me his bruised hand. "Hand." I demanded.

Jack raised his eyebrows at my tone, but I caught a twitch upward at the corner of his mouth that he tried to conceal. He gave me his hand and I saw him try to hide his wince as I held the ice to his bruised knuckles that were already a lovely shade of purple. He looked down into my eyes. "What did he want, Syd?"

"He tried to apologize and tell me that we belonged together and he wants me back." My voice was low.

Jack closed his eyes for a minute and I waited

anxiously for his response to come. "Do you want to go back to him?"

"What?" I was shocked he would even ask such a thing. "No! I can't even stand to look at him! It took me a while to realize it, but I never really belonged with him."

Jack took the ice pack from my hand and tossed it on the counter behind him. He took my hands in his and pulled them behind my back, securing them with his as he pulled me tightly against him. "Who do you belong to, Syd?"

My heart melted knowing that such a strong, controlling man needed my reassurance.

"You, Jack."

"Say it, Syd." He pulled me tighter so that there was no air between our bodies.

My heart fluttered wildly. I knew it was true, but I hadn't admitted it out loud. My voice was a whisper as I looked up at him. "I belong to you."

Jack's grip on my hands behind my back tightened. His pale green eyes turned almost gray, dark and wild. "Say it again. Louder."

I raised my voice and matched his gaze. "I belong to you."

His lips covered mine urgently and our mouths slid harshly as our tongues collided with insatiable need. He lifted me up and I wrapped my legs around his waist. I felt his hardness pressing into me and I unwittingly gasped. My reaction drew him into even more of a frenzy. His hand on my ass pulled me into him as our kiss deepened nearly into violence. His other hand wrapped in my hair and he forced us apart purposefully. "Say it again."

I was breathless and panting. "I belong to you, Jack."

He growled and I felt his hand dive between my legs, sliding his fingers under my underwear, quickly finding my clit with his thumb. He pushed down gently and massaged small rapid circles. I knew he was making sure I was ready to take him. Even in his own frenzied state he put my needs before his own. When he was sure I was wet and ready, he turned us so that my ass rested against the countertop as he opened his pants, freeing his enormous erection.

I felt the wide crest of his cock at my entrance and I tried desperately to free my hands from his strong hold behind my back, desperate to touch it, desperate to glide my hands up and down its massive length. But my attempt was fruitless under Jack's strong grip. He circled his hips with just the crest inside of me and I arched my back trying to pull him deeper inside of me, but Jack's other hand pinned me in place where he wanted me. "Again," he commanded.

"I belong to you. Only you." My cry was desperate. I needed him inside of me so badly it was painful. But my response was raw and full of emotion and earned me what I wanted. Jack thrust into me deeply, stretching me wide as he filled me to his root. He grinded deeply inside of me, desperate to go further. "Again." His voice was throaty and deep.

"You, I belong to you, only you."

Jack held me in place, restraining my movement and pumping deep and hard into me as if his life depended on filling me. His constant, rhythmic pounding over and over, deeper and deeper, had me panting wildly and I was on the edge of what I knew would be a wild, soaring orgasm. I shut my eyes and began to let it wash over me as he continued his brutal thrusts.

"Open your eyes."

My eyes flew open to meet his. "Again."

My orgasm ripped through me at his command. "I belong," I moaned, unable to finish the sentence in one breath. His rhythm quickened and I knew he was unable to hold back much longer. "To you...." The last two words came out in a scream as the orgasm completely washed over my body, shaking me to my core. I felt the heat of Jack's semen run through me as he emptied his body and filled mine. He growled my name and my body collapsed spinelessly into his arms.

I was vaguely aware of Jack carrying me to the bedroom and covering me up, but I was exhausted and emotionally drained and my body needed to escape to rest.

The next morning I was surprised to find Jack next to me when I woke. We had established a routine of him getting up while I slept and me going to find him in his office hours later. "You're still in bed." I smiled and snuggled closer to him.

He spoke with his lips in my hair as he kissed the top of my head. "I couldn't leave you this morning."

I knew what he meant. I needed him next to me that morning after the night we'd had too. "I'm glad you couldn't," I said softly.

I rested my head on his naked chest, playing with the smattering of hair, twirling it between my fingers. "My mom is coming down for a visit next weekend."

His hand had been stroking my hair and stopped in its place. "Do you want me to meet her?"

I thought about the question before asking. "I don't think I have a choice. I sort of mentioned I met someone and she started an interrogation over the phone. If she doesn't get to meet you, she won't sleep for a month."

Jack laughed lightly and I was relieved that he didn't seem bothered by my response. "Where is she staying?"

I hadn't thought about it. My apartment was small, but she could share my bed with me for a night or two and deal with the close space. Although there would be absolutely no escaping her inquisition in such a small area. "My place, I guess. We didn't really talk about it."

"I'll book you a suite here so you can each have your own bedroom. I'll tell the manager to book you both a day at the spa so you can relax and get pampered together."

I raised my head to look at him. "That's very sweet, but I couldn't ask you to do that."

"You didn't ask, I offered, and I want to do it. Plus, I have my own secret agenda. It keeps you closer to me and butters up your mom for me."

I laughed. "I can't imagine any woman would need any buttering for them to not fall head over heels for you."

Jack rolled on top of me playfully. "Is that so?"

"You're a mother's dream, tall, dark and handsome, good manners, straight teeth and wealthy."

"What about her daughter's dream. How am I doing there?"

"Fulfilling them all." I lifted my head to kiss him softly.

Chapter 20

The next week flew by and I was surprised that I was actually looking forward to my mom's visit. Lyle had complained, but gave me Saturday night off, and the thought of staying at the Heston Grand and having all day spa treatments with my mom was exciting. At first my mother balked at the idea of staying at a hotel, but then I filled her in on Jack and his hotels and she warmed to the idea quickly. She sounded excited to visit and I realized that I had missed her and was excited to see her too.

Jack had insisted on Mateo picking up my mom Saturday morning and had arranged what sounded like an amazing day. Brunch in Café Dumo, the hotel's five star restaurant, followed by massages, manicures and pedicures, and wash and blow outs at the Luxor Spa. He had booked us into the Presidential Suite, one floor below his penthouse, which occupied the entire top floor.

Jack gave me the key to the suite Saturday morning and told me that he had work to do all day and would meet us at our room at seven, before dinner. I took the elevator down one floor and found the entire floor had suites named after presidents. Each single door had a carved sign with a president's name and a silhouette of the president's profile. Following the signs for the presidential suite, I passed Ford, Lincoln, Washington and Kennedy. As I passed the Kennedy suite, I remembered that Jack had said that he kept a "sex suite" and wondered if one of them was his secret love shack. Perhaps the Kennedy suite? After all, his name was Jack and he was known as the womanizing president. I hated the thought of Jack's suite seeping into my brain to darken the day after all that Jack had done to make the day perfect for my mom and I.

I arrived at the double door presidential suite and slipped in the key to open it. The smell of fresh flowers hit me immediately as I entered. The suite was beautiful and enormous. Floor to ceiling windows overlooking Manhattan, glistening white marble floors and three huge bouquets of all white roses sat in sparkling crystal vases spread across the grand living room. To the right was a working fireplace, with a huge wooden carved mirror hanging above the mantle. To the left was a dining room, a small kitchen, and a long hallway, which I assumed led to the bedrooms.

I had expected the suite to be nice, but it was beyond anything that I could have imagined. It hadn't dawned on me that the suite was truly a presidential suite and had likely housed actual presidents in the past. I walked to the dining room table where a card was perched on one of the vases that housed at least two dozen roses. I opened the card, recognizing Jack's handwriting immediately. *Syd, Hope you enjoy the suite. The thought of you being so close, yet not in our bed, is going to kill me tonight. Jack.*

Holy. Shit. *Our bed.* Did he even realize that he'd written it? My heart swelled at the thought that Jack thought of his bed as our bed. I was falling deeper and deeper for the incredible man and all of the little thoughtful things that he did for me. He made me feel taken care of on so many levels, physically, emotionally and definitely sexually. As I looked around the suite, feeling engulfed by Jack. I realized that what he needed to hear from me was true. I belonged to him.

By the end of the day I felt like a princess. I knew the spa was exclusive and expected good service, but Jack had made sure that my every need was taken care of. I was positive that the staff had to have been advised of who I was because they couldn't possibly be that attentive to every customer every day in the same way as they were to my mom and I. We sipped champagne and wore plush robes that were embroidered with our initials and were truly treated like royalty. The young girl that did my manicure was sweet, but chatty. She told me that the spa had brought in one of the top celebrity stylists for our blowouts and that Mr. Heston had selected our masseuses personally. I was impressed, but not surprised, at the lengths to which Jack had gone. I was starting to realize that one of the reasons that he was so successful was that he didn't do anything halfway.

I hadn't even realized that the suite had a doorbell until it rang promptly at 7pm. Of course I was running late and Jack was right on time. I opened the door and flung my arms around his neck, giving him a big kiss and hug. Jack smiled down at me. "What was that for?"

"It was for being the best boyfriend ever. We had the best day. Thank you, baby." I reached up on my tippy toes and kissed him again gently on the lips.

"Well, I really hope that you are, Jack, with the kind of welcome you just got." I heard my mom speak from behind me and blushed at the thought of what she had just watched me do. I must have looked like a schoolgirl running up to the boy that she had a crush on.

Jack smiled his insanely perfect smile, extending his hand with one arm and keeping the other wrapped tightly around my waist. "You must be Mrs. St. Claire. It's a pleasure to meet you."

Good God, I decided right there and then that my children were going to the same boarding school that Jack had attended, just so they could come out with his incredibly alluring manners.

Mom shook Jack's hand and I could swear she blushed a little bit as she said, "Call me Renee, please."

"Renee." Jack nodded and released her hand.

"Go get ready, honey, you are always late. I won't tell Jack too many stories about your childhood if you hurry." Mom laughed, but I knew she wasn't kidding.

I gave her a silent 'I'll kill you if you do' face as I walked by and then rushed to finish getting ready. I heard Jack and mom laughing a few times in the other room and, although I was afraid of what horrible childhood stories she was sharing, the sound of them laughing together warmed my heart.

Jack stood as I entered the room. The only time the man didn't have perfect manners was in the bedroom. In the bedroom he was domineering and commanding, such a stark contrast in some ways to the please-and-thank-you gentleman that stood before me. Although, if I really thought about it, both bedroom and gentlemanly Jack had one thing in common: they took care of me.

Dinner was incredible, even though mom shared too many embarrassing childhood stories. She told Jack about my penchant for streaking when I was four, and about the time that I took off all my clothes and rode my bicycle down the entire block naked. Apparently, I had only made it about a dozen houses before the old lady next door called to report that she was upset at my lewd behavior. I knew from Jack's face during that particular story that I'd be hearing more about my little naked endeavors later.

Mom didn't grill Jack as bad as I thought she would, but she seemed satisfied at the answers she got to the questions she did ask. The glass of wine with dinner, coupled with the massage earlier in the day and how well things were going, allowed me to relax. But my relaxation didn't last long. Every muscle jumped back into a tight ball of stress the minute I saw Jack's father walk into the restaurant. I silently said a prayer that he wouldn't see us, but God wasn't listening.

Jack's back was to the door, so he had no warning until he was standing beside our table. "Sydney, how nice to see you." I watched as Jack's face changed, his smiling eyes shuttered, and his jaw tensed as he turned with a face of steel. "Son, it wasn't enough to take out one pretty girl this evening, you had to bring her sister too?"

Shit. I had to do something. If Jack had to say more than two words to his father I knew it wasn't going to end pretty. I jumped in headfirst, "This is my mom, Renee, Mr. Heston." My mom turned to face Jack's dad and I watched her take him in. He was an older, more polished-looking version of Jack. Jack was sexy with chiseled features, but there was still something about him that was rough and rugged. His dad, on the other hand, screamed old money and polish and didn't look like he'd ever had a fistfight in his life. But he was still a very handsome older man, a fact clearly not lost on my mother.

"Didn't I tell you to call me Jack, Sydney? The way you two have been inseparable lately, you might be calling me Dad one day." His father winked at me with his comment.

Jack's father held out his hand to my mother and I thought Jack was going to explode when he brought my mother's hand to his mouth and gently kissed the top of her hand. Luckily my aim was good, and my foot met Jack's shin under the table just as he was pushing his chair back to get up. He looked at me and I sent him warning eyes, begging him to stay put. I was shocked that he listened.

My mother blushed a bit "Nice to meet you, Mr. Heston."

"You too, my dear. I can see where Syd gets her beauty from."

Shit, Shit, Shit. From the look on Jack's face, I knew he was about to blow and I had to do something quick. I stood awkwardly. "It was nice to see you Mr. Heston, umm Jack, you'll have to excuse me. I was just going to go the ladies room before you walked over. Mom, why don't you join me?"

Mom looked disappointed to be dragged away from the debonair Jack Heston Sr., but she stood to go nonetheless. "It was nice meeting you, Mr. Heston." My mom shook his hand again and I nodded, knowing a physical touch from his father to me could send Jack right over the edge.

"Be right back, Jack." I smiled and widened my eyes to Jack, another attempt at a warning.

I took as long as I could in the bathroom, trying to wait out whatever storm had to come to pass in the restaurant. My mom didn't seem to notice anything unusual about Jack's dad's visit to our table, or, if she did, she didn't say anything. Either way, I was grateful not to have to explain anything to her. I reapplied my lipstick, stalling for time, and then took a deep breath as we made our way back to our table. I was relieved to find Jack's father gone and didn't dare look around the restaurant for him, for fear finding him would cause him to reappear. Jack was sitting at the table and I noticed he had an empty small cut crystal glass in front of him that hadn't been there earlier. As we sat, I realized that he had ordered a drink and downed it while we were in the restroom.

"I ordered us dessert to be delivered to my suite. Renee said she wanted to see my floor." His voice was harder than it had been earlier, but I knew he was trying for me.

I mouthed 'thank you' to him and he responded with a small smile and nod of the head.

Jack kept his hand at the small of my back and didn't look back as we walked out of the restaurant. I saw his dad out of the corner of my eye, sitting at a table with a woman who looked at least twenty years his junior.

After dessert and a grand tour of his penthouse, Jack walked my mom and I back to the presidential suite. My mom graciously said goodnight and went to her room to give us a few minutes of privacy.

"You okay? You had me scared there for a few minutes when I saw your face when your father stopped by our table."

"I'll deal with him later." He buried his head in my hair and nibbled on my neck.

I giggled. "Stop, my mother is in the next room."

"You could sneak upstairs after she goes to sleep," Jack teased as he continued trailing kisses down my neck.

I ducked out of his reach. "No way. I think she really likes you. I'm not messing that up," I teased playfully as I walked around him and started to push him towards the door.

Jack turned at the door and took my face in his hands. "You think she likes me?" He could be so irresistibly adorable when he wanted to.

"Yes, I think she loves you."

"I've never met a woman's mother before."

I'd forgotten that he didn't have any relationship experience and that things like meeting my parents would be first experiences to him. He'd just seemed so confident and secure that it was easy to forget that it was new for him. I adored that he cared if she liked him and that he was nervous about it. If it was possible, it made him even more endearing to me.

"Well, mine loved you." I reached up on my tippy-toes and kissed his nose.

Jack kissed me chastely goodnight and I watched him walk down the hall. I could have sworn that he looked at the Kennedy suite and then back to me, confirming what I had wondered just the day before.

Chapter 21

Saturday night I didn't mind going to work, but only because I knew Jack and Sienna were coming to the club. Sienna was bringing a few friends from her band and I was surprised when Jack had agreed to join them. Sienna had told me to invite Jack, but I never actually expected him to say yes.

Sienna and her friends arrived first, and I could tell that the party wasn't just getting started, it had been underway for at least a few hours. They were rowdy and loud, but it was just what the club needed. Sienna was clad in one of her usual club hopping outfits, four-inch high-heeled black leather boots that came to her knees, a black leather mini skirt, and a tight black Sinners concert t-shirt emblazoned with red sparkling sequins. I picked a song I knew she couldn't resist and watched as she made her way to the dance floor. By the time the song ended, the number of people on the dance floor had doubled. Sienna's energy could get a party at a funeral started.

I couldn't resist calling Sienna to the stage for a song. Of course, it didn't take much to get her to oblige. I couldn't remember Sienna ever turning down an opportunity to sing since we were kids. It didn't matter where or when, she was always ready for a performance. I told the band what song to sing and the two of us took turns singing different parts. We hadn't practiced the song together in years, but neither one hesitated when it was our part to sing. It just came naturally to sing with Sienna, as it always did since third grade. As we dove into the chorus, singing in perfect harmony together, I saw Jack watching us from the bar. I smiled at him and he smiled back as he raised his glass to me.

The crowd loved our performance and I knew it was a bad time to take a set break. I should have kept the energy going by singing another dance song. But I wanted to say hi to the beautiful man on the other side of the room and show Sienna to the booth that I had reserved for them.

Jack didn't move as I walked in his direction, and his eyes never left me. I looked up to his gorgeous face as I walked, captured by his green eyes sparkling in the semidarkness of the club. His focus on me was searing. I didn't say a word and neither did he. Instead my mouth reached up and went for his. It took less than two seconds for Jack to regain control of the kiss that I had started. He took my face in his hands and held my face where he wanted it as he kissed me senseless.

By the time he broke the kiss my knees were weak. I was in the middle of the club where I worked and the man had me panting and breathless in twenty seconds flat. I should have known better than to start anything remotely sexual with Jack in public.

"You looked like you were having a great time up there." Jack's thumb rubbed my bottom lip as he spoke.

I took a deep breath to regain my wits. "I was. I really do love singing with Sienna."

Sienna broke into our cocoon, the sarcasm dripping from her voice. "I'd say get a room, but you already have a whole hotel full of them, don't you?"

Jack and I both turned to Sienna. "I do. But I have to warn off the hungry masses of men drooling at the two of you on stage somehow, don't I? Jack's words were said in jest, but I knew there was an element of truth in them. He was definitely an alpha dog that marked his territory to keep the pack at bay.

"Well, don't keep the masses from me, I don't have a prince charming of my own to sweep me off my feet at the end of the night yet." Sienna winked and reached up and kissed Jack on the cheek.

Jack shook his head and smiled and Sienna introduced us to her friends. Some of them I already knew from the band, but there were a few new faces. After a few minutes, I excused myself and went back to rejoin the band. The night went by quickly and I loved watching my friends dance and enjoy my music. I tried not to focus on Jack, but I couldn't help myself. I couldn't be in a room with him and not watch him. And I caught him watching me on more than just a few occasions too.

The next afternoon I laid in bed with a bit of a hangover from the tequila shots I'd had with Sienna after I finished working. My head dangled sideways at the foot of the bed, the covers pulled up to my neck. An hour earlier, Jack had moved from his office and sat with his back against the headboard, typing on the keyboard of the laptop on his lap. "Do you really like this movie?"

I turned to look at him. I loved to see him that way, wearing a simple white t-shirt and jeans and his feet crossed at the ankles, his long legs splayed down the length of the bed. He looked so young and relaxed. I knew that it wasn't a side of him that many people knew. "It's a classic. Who doesn't love *Ghost*?"

"Babe, men don't like *Ghost*."

"They don't?"

"No, they don't."

"And you speak for all men?" I rose an eyebrow inquisitively.

"I do."

I crawled up the bed, straddling his legs. "What do men like then?"

Jack grinned and folded down his laptop.

"You, naked and the TV off."

I pressed my pelvis down and felt his erection stabbing into my cleft. "Is that all men, or just you?" I teased as I rolled my hips.

Jack leaned up and firmly gripped my ribcage. "There will be no other men seeing you naked."

I leaned in and bit his ear gently before I whispered, "Because I belong to you."

The following Monday was Jack's birthday and I wanted to surprise him, but what do you get a man with unlimited resources and a personal shopper with exquisite taste? I struggled for almost a week and decided on a gift with meaning instead of something from a store that I couldn't really afford and he didn't really want. I was sure it was a great idea, until I was on my way to his office to surprise him with it, then I thought it was a stupid gift and I would embarrass myself.

The guard greeted me at the door and recognized me from my earlier visit with Jack. I told him I wanted to surprise Jack for his birthday. He was hesitant to let me in, but did it anyway when I reassured him that it was okay. I passed a few people on the way to Jack's office door. All of them said hello and seemed to remember me. I was feeling confident until I stood in front his closed office door. I suddenly felt like an intruder and wasn't sure if I should knock or walk in. I decided to knock.

Jack yelled to come in and I opened the door. He was leaning against the front of his desk with his arms folded and Jenna sat in front of him, too close for my liking. His face showed surprise at my visit, but he made no attempt to hide anything he was doing. Jenna turned and saw me, giving me a cunning smile.

"Syd, is everything okay?"

I took a few steps inside, suddenly feeling sick to my stomach. "I … I … I just wanted to surprise you with a birthday present. But I see that you're busy. I'm sorry I interrupted." I put the wrapped package down on the couch in his office and turned for the door, desperately needing to get out of there. It was suddenly as if all the air in the building had been sucked out and I needed to make it outside for my next breath.

Jack caught me at the end of the hall, grabbing onto my arm. "Syd, what's going on? Where are you going?"

I couldn't turn to look at him for fear I would lose it. All of the memories came flashing back from the day that I'd walked into Michael's office and found him leaning against his desk, his secretary on her knees, her head bobbing as she took him in. I struggled to free myself from Jack's grip and ran as fast as I could to my car.

Jack stopped calling after the first day. I don't know why I wouldn't return his calls. I knew I was acting childish, but I wasn't ready to speak to him. I couldn't even bring myself to listen to his voicemails. Three days later I was still dragging myself around feeling sick and sorry for myself. I had dark circles under my eyes and my face was swollen from crying. My hair was matted from the tossing and turning the night before and I didn't have the desire to brush it. I forced myself to undress and turned on the hot water to steam up my tiny bathroom. The knock at the front door startled me, as I was about to step into the shower.

I threw on my robe and went to the door to find Jack on the other side.

"What do you want?" My voice was low and lackluster.

Jack stepped inside, closing the door behind him. "I don't know what the fuck I did, but I'm going crazy, Syd." I looked up at him, seeing him for the first time in three days. He looked like I felt. The impeccably groomed man with the pale sparkling eyes was a disheveled mess. He had three days of scruff and his skin was sallow and eyes dim.

"I can't do this, Jack." My voice was a whisper and the words began to break as I spoke. Jack took a step toward me and I put my hand up, keeping him at distance.

"What can't you do, Syd?" His tone was angry and he took another step closer.

I took another step back and spoke to his chest. "I can't close my eyes and not see what is going on around me just because it makes life easier for me."

Jack took another step closer and lifted my chin, forcing me to look at him. "Look at me. What do you think is going on?"

I looked away and didn't respond. I was fighting the tears back with all my might and I couldn't look into his eyes.

He let go of my face and raked both his hands through his hair in frustration. Then he took a deep breath and grabbed my face with both hands, bringing himself down to my eye level. I had nowhere to look but into his eyes. "Nothing is going on and you know it. You're scared. And so the fuck am I." He paused and searched my eyes. "Baby, I'm not him. I'm not the asshole that made you afraid of giving yourself to me, but I wish like hell I could take away what he did to you. Because I'm in. I'm all in, baby. I'm not perfect and I don't know what the fuck I did to deserve someone as good as you, but you have me and I'm not settling for just a part of you. I want you. I want all of you, baby."

The tears flooded my eyes and poured down my face. Jack pulled me close to him and held me until there were no more tears left.

I pulled my face out of his chest. "There's nothing going on between you and Jenna?" I looked up at him raw, vulnerability on the table bared to him.

"There's only you, baby." Jack paused and reached down and lifted me up, cradling me into his arms. "I belong to you."

Chapter 22

Weeks passed and my angst about Jack's other life and the people he shared it with began to subside. We began to fall back into a routine and we even went out with Jack's friend Tyler that I'd met in Hawaii and his new girlfriend a few times. We were beginning to settle in as a couple and, although it scared me, I was happier than I had ever been in my life.

Sunday morning we were reading the paper in bed when my cell phone rang and flashed a picture of Sienna. "Hey." I didn't even get to finish the word, Sienna was already talking over me. I had to ask her to slow down just to be able to make out what she was saying. Her voice was screeching with excitement and she was going a mile a minute. I was only able to make out the last sentence. "The Smiths, Syd, can you believe it!"

I was confused and my conversation had gotten Jack's attention too. He looked at me silently, asking if everything was alright, and I shrugged my shoulders in response. "What about the Smiths?"

Sienna took a deep breath to calm her on the phone. "They want us to open for them, Syd! They want us, me and you, us, to open for them!"

"What, when?" I loved the Smiths. Years ago, when Sienna and I had a band back in Boston, we had made friends with a lot of other local bands; one of them was the Smiths. We had a mutual respect for each other's music and we had always joked that someday we would alternate opening for each other's bands when we went on tour. Years later, the Smiths made it big and Sienna and I were happy that, if it couldn't have been us, we were glad it was them. Sienna and I had been to a dozen concerts over the last few years and I knew they were about to release another album.

"On their tour, Syd." Her voice was elevating back to screaming. "They want us to open for them for their whole tour!"

"I didn't even know they had a tour set up here anytime soon."

"They don't. It's a European tour, Syd. Four months of singing and traveling through Europe with the Smiths! Can. You. Fucking. Believe it!"

I held the phone away from my ear as she continued to scream. Oh. My. God. It was my dream come true. I had no idea how it had happened, but it was every musicians dream. I turned and looked at Jack and suddenly my heart was in my throat. I saw in his face that he'd overheard the news that Syd had just shared. How could he not have, she was screaming every word.

Sienna blabbered on and on, as I struggled to keep my composure on the phone with her. I felt like I was just punched in the stomach and the wind was knocked out of me. I was thrilled and excited, but scared and sickened at the same time. "When does it start?" I had to feign excitement, but it broke my heart as Jack rose from the bed and went into the living room.

"A week?" I was exasperated. "When do they need an answer?"

"An answer?" Sienna laughed. "I already gave them one! Of course we are doing this, Syd!"

A few minutes later I was able to get Sienna off the phone and found Jack standing against the window, looking out over the city. I wrapped my arms around his back and hugged him tightly. Neither of us said anything for a few minutes.

"When do you leave?" Jack turned to face me, clasping his arms around my back.

"In a week. It's a four month European tour."

I caught Jack's jaw tense, but he tried to hide it from me. He brushed my hair back from my face. "Congratulations, Syd. It's your dream come true."

I thought about his words. He was right. It was my dream come true, but why did it feel like my worst nightmare? "Thank you. I think I need some time to process it all."

A few days passed and Jack and I went about our lives as usual. We talked about the tour schedule, the travel plans, and the venues we would play, but we steered clear of the thing we both needed to talk about most. Us. What would my leaving do to us? Would we be able to survive as a couple with months of not seeing other? Would we even try a long distance relationship? I wasn't sure why we hadn't talked about it yet, but I was terrified of the answers that needed to be said.

Two days before I was to leave, I woke up to find Jack in his home office, working. I couldn't leave without having the conversation, no matter how much I dreaded having it. I sat on the other side of his desk, something I had never done before. The only place I ever sat in Jack's office was on his lap. Jack looked up at me and waited for me to speak.

"What's going to happen to us when I go, Jack?"

Jack stopped what he was doing and his hands rubbed his forehead. "What do you want to happen, Syd?"

"I don't want to go, Jack. I'm afraid to leave you, I don't want to lose you." A tear escaped before I could stop it.

"I don't want you to go either, Syd. But you have to. When we first met in Hawaii you said yourself that you had forgotten who you were when you were with Michael. You need to do this for you. It's your dream."

He came around the desk and lifted me, setting me down on top of his lap. "I'll come to Europe to see you and you can come home when you have a few days between shows." His face was serious and his tone was unwavering.

I knew he was right, but it didn't make it hurt any less. I looked into his eyes and saw his sacrifice. "I love you, Jack." I hadn't planned to say it, the words just came out on their own.

Jack lifted me up and carried me to the bedroom, setting me down on the bed gently. I watched as he unbuckled his pants and took off his boxers, never taking his eyes off of me. He sat me up and pulled the tank-top I was wearing over my head. He climbed on top of me and gently kissed my lips. He pulled his head back just enough to look me in the eyes. "I love you too, Syd." Then he made love to me.

On the morning of my flight, I was surprised that Jack said he needed to stop at the office. "I just have to pick up something. We can stop on the way to the airport. It will only take five minutes."

We were both quiet, but it didn't have anything to do with the unplanned stop at Jack's office. I wasn't going to see Jack for three full weeks, until I had a break in my schedule. We planned for him to fly to Rome for four days then. He was going to come for the Rome concert and then we were going to stay three days together, before I had to fly out to Prague for the next show.

Mateo pulled up in front of Jack's office and he opened the door and held out his hand. I was surprised that he wanted me to come inside, after the last time I had visited. I really didn't want his last memory of me in his office to be my childish behavior from last time, so I sucked it up and got out with him without question.

Jack's assistant spied us as soon as we walked in. "It's on your desk." She smiled at me sweetly.

We walked to his office hand in hand. I was relieved that I didn't have any Jenna sightings that might upset me before I had to leave. Inside his office, Jack handed me an envelope.

"What's this?"

"Open it."

Inside was a pretty silver heart keychain with a bunch of keys and some folded papers.

I looked at him curiously.

"The keys to the penthouse, my office, and the storage unit. And an open first class ticket in case you need to come home for an unplanned visit."

I understood the first two and the last. "The storage unit?" I asked, confused.

"Where I'm having your furniture stored next weekend. I'm moving you into the penthouse next weekend. You can figure out what you want to keep and get rid of when you get back."

My eyes widened with disbelief. I was about to argue when, out the corner of my eye, I saw the picture that I had given him on his desk, perfectly positioned for him to see from his chair. He had taken the present I had rudely delivered to him on his birthday and put it proudly on display. My picture was on the desk of the man who never had any personal belongings in his office. I took a deep breath and decided to throw caution to the wind. "Okay."

"Okay?" He had definitely expected more of an argument.

I reached up on my tippy toes and kissed him sweetly on the mouth. "I belong to you, so why not."

Jack tipped my head back and kissed me deeply. "I'm going to be taking a lot of cold showers over the next three weeks." He made a sexy growling noise as he took both my ass cheeks into his hands and pressed me up against his erection. For the first time in a week, I felt like we might actually make it. We might.....

Jack and Sydney's story
continues in book two,
Made for You.

Other Books by Vi Keeland

Life on Stage series (2 standalone books)
Beat
Throb

MMA Fighter series (3 standalone books)
Worth the Fight
Worth the Chance
Worth Forgiving

The Cole Series (2 book serial)
Belong to You
Made for You

Standalone novels
Bossman
The Baller
Stuck-Up Suit (Co-written with Penelope Ward)
Cocky Bastard (Co-written with Penelope Ward)
Playboy Pilot (Co-written with Penelope Ward)
Left Behind (A Young Adult Novel)
First Thing I See

Lightning Source UK Ltd.
Milton Keynes UK
UKHW010643120421
381850UK00002B/392